ABOUT THE AUTHOR

Barbara Cartland, the world's most famous romantic novelist, who is also an historian, playwright, lecturer, political speaker and television personality, has now written over 460 books and sold nearly 500 million all over the world.

She has also had many historical works published and has written four autobiographies as well as the biographies of her mother and that of her brother, Ronald Cartland, who was the first Member of Parliament to be killed in the Second World War. This book has a preface by Sir Winston Churchill and has just been republished with an introduction by the late Sir Arthur Bryant.

Love at the Helm, a novel written with the help and inspiration of the late Earl Mountbatten of Burma, Great Uncle of His Royal Highness The Prince of Wales, is being sold for the Mountbatten Memorial Trust.

She has broken the world record for the last twelve years by writing an average of twenty-three books a year. In the Guinness Book of Records she is listed as the world's top-selling author.

Miss Cartland in 1978 sang an Album of Love Songs with the Royal Philharmonic orchestra.

In private life Barbara Cartland, who is a Dame of Grace of the Order of St. John of Jerusalem, Chairman of the St. John Council in Hertfordshire and Deputy President of the St. John Ambulance Brigade, has fought for better conditions and salaries for Midwives and Nurses.

She championed the cause for the Elderly, in 1956 invoking a Government Enquiry into the "Housing Conditions of Old People".

In 1962 she had the Law of England changed so that Local Authorities had to provide camps for their own Gypsies. This has meant that since then thousands and thousands of Gypsy children have been able to go to School which they had never been able to do in the past, as their caravans were moved every twenty-four hours by the Police.

There are now fourteen camps in Hertfordshire and Barbara Cartland has her own Romany Gypsy Camp called Barbaraville by the Gypsies.

Her designs "Decorating with Love" are being sold all over

the U.S.A. and the National Home Fashions League made her, in 1981, "Woman of Achievement".

Barbara Cartland's book *Getting Older, Growing Younger* has been published in Great Britain and the U.S.A. and her fifth Cookery Book, *The Romance of Food*, is now being used by the House of Commons.

In 1984 she received, at Kennedy Airport, America's Bishop Wright Air Industry Award for her contribution to the development of aviation. In 1931 she and two R.A.F. Officers thought of, and carried, the first aeroplane-towed glider air-mail.

During the War she was Chief Lady Welfare Officer in Bedfordshire looking after 20,000 Service men and women. She thought of having a pool of Wedding Dresses at the War Office so a Service Bride could hire a gown for the day.

She bought 1,000 gowns without coupons for the A.T.S., the W.A.A.F.s and the W.R.E.N.s. In 1945 Barbara Cartland received the Certificate of Merit from Eastern Command.

In 1964 Barbara Cartland founded the National Association for Health of which she is President, as a front for all the Health Stores and for any product made as alternative medicine.

This is now a £300,000 turnover a year industry, with one third going in export.

In January 1988 she received "La Medaille de Vermeil de la Ville de Paris" (the Gold Medal of Paris). This is the highest award to be given in France by the City of Paris for Achievement – twenty-five million books sold in France.

THE LOVELY LIAR

The Countess of Ravensdale runs away from her husband with a fascinating, but compulsive gambler and when he dies she is left penniless.

She and her daughter Noella seek help from her cousin, Mrs. Wakefield and her daughter, who is also called Noella.

For a short while they are happy, then a friend arrives from Africa who infects them with a fever for which the doctors have no cure.

Both the Countess and her daughter die, and when Mrs. Wakefield also dies from the same illness, Noella is all alone.

Noella who is exactly like her namesake in appearance is on the verge of starvation with her old Nurse, and Hawkins, a manservant.

The Earl of Ravensdale has died and when his son Lyndon inherits the title, he sends his Cousin Jasper to find his sister.

Because Jasper is financially involved in the search, when he discovers that the Earl's sister is dead, he persuades Noella, against her better judgement, to take her place.

How Noella, ashamed of her lies and deceit, travels to Yorkshire and meets her supposed brother.

How she is blackmailed by Jasper and how he threatens her life, is all told in this dramatic story of deep emotions, and is the 409th book by Barbara Cartland.

BARBARA CARTLAND

THE LOVELY LIAR

Pan Original
Pan Books London, Sydney and Auckland

First published 1988 by Pan Books Ltd,
Cavaye Place, London SW10 9PG
9 8 7 6 5 4 3 2 1
© Cartland Promotions 1988
ISBN 0 330 30399 6
Photoset by Parker Typesetting Service, Leicester
Printed in Great Britain by
Richard Clay Ltd

Author's Note

The beautiful county of Yorkshire has many great ancestral houses among its hills and dales and the most magnificent is Castle Howard.

It was recently the background of a Television film:
"Brideshead Revisited", and its magnificence when one
first sees it is breathtaking.

Horace Walpole described it better than I can when he
writes:

> *"Nobody informed me that at one view I should see a
> Palace, a town, a fortified City, temples on high places,
> woods being beech, meeting place of Druids."*

Another house of great importance where the Princess
Royal wife of the Earl of Harewood, lived for many years,
is Harewood.

I think the most attractive room in the house is the
Music Room which I have described in this novel.

Having lived in such exquisite surroundings, it is not
surprising that the present 7th Earl is closely connected
with the Royal Opera House at Covent Garden, and has
directed both in the Leeds and the Edinburgh Festivals.

Chapter One
1835

Noella looked around the room with a despairing expression in her eyes.

It was horrifying to think of how much it had altered since she could first remember it.

There were marks on the walls where the pictures had once hung, and the mirror over the mantelpiece had gone.

So had the pretty French desk at which her mother had always sat to write her letters.

All that was left was a sofa of which the springs were broken, two arm-chairs that were very shabby, and a carpet.

That was so threadbare it would not be worth taking off the floor.

Everything else had been sold and Noella knew there was nothing left in the room that would fetch even a few shillings.

She walked to the window to look out at the untidy overgrown garden.

There were still the flowers that her mother had planted coming into bud in the Spring.

There were daffodils, golden under the trees, but because there was no one to tend the lawn, it was not the smooth green she remembered.

Brambles had grown over the shrubs and their Spring blossom was struggling for life against them.

"What am I to do?" she asked.

Then as there was no answer she said with a little sob:

"Oh . . Mama . . help me . . please . . help me!"

It seemed incredible that everything should have happened so quickly and that she was, almost before she realised it, completely alone in the world.

When her father retired from his Regiment after a distinguished career in which he had been awarded a medal for gallantry, he had been granted a generous pension.

He had died from more than one of the wounds he had received in battle, although they had taken a long time to kill him.

His widow had then received half the pension that he had enjoyed during his lifetime.

Because the house had always seemed carefree and full of love, Noella had never thought of asking what would happen to her if her mother died.

At the back of her mind she had expected long before her mother grew old, to be married and have a husband to protect and look after her.

After the first shock of losing her husband, whom she had adored, Mrs. Wakefield had tried to make her daughter happy.

She was also determined to make sure she should be well educated.

Every penny that could be spared during her husband's lifetime had been spent on Noella who had in consequence, been taught many more subjects than was ordinarily considered necessary for girls of her age.

She was extremely intelligent and benefited from everything she learnt.

Her teachers were the Vicar who was a very erudite man, a retired School-Master, and a Governess who had been for many years with an aristocratic family.

Noella loved reading and, as her mother often said, 'travelled in her mind' to all sorts of strange places in every part of the world.

There was practically no social life in the quiet country village in Worcestershire, where on his retirement, her father had bought a house very cheaply.

It was an ancient black-and-white timbered house and Noella had always thought it beautiful and it had always seemed to her full of sunshine and laughter.

Even after her mother became a widow they would laugh together in the evenings when Noella had finished her lessons.

They would tell each other stories in which having found a treasure in the garden they were able to travel, to the places about which Noella had read and which had captured her imagination.

Then, a year ago, when she was seventeen, her mother's cousin, Caroline Ravensdale, had arrived unexpectedly with her daughter.

Mrs. Wakefield had often talked to Noella about her cousin of whom she was very fond, as they were the same age and had grown up together.

Mrs. Wakefield had told Noella about their childhood, but she was sixteen before she learnt the truth about Caroline Ravensdale.

Caroline, it appeared, whose father was much richer than her mother's family, had been taken to London for the Season.

There because she was so beautiful, she had been an instantaneous success.

"She had hair the same colour as yours, my dearest," Mrs. Wakefield said to Noella, "which come from a Swedish ancestor far back in our history, and recurs from time to time in succeeding generations."

Noella's hair was the very pale gold of the sun when it first appears over the horizon, but her eyes were not the sky-blue that might have been expected.

They were the deep blue of a stormy sea.

"Caroline was so much acclaimed in London," Mrs. Wakefield went on, "that nobody was surprised when she made a brilliant marriage."

"Who did she marry, Mama?" Noella had asked the first time she had heard the story.

"The Earl of Ravensdale," her mother replied. "He

11

was much older than she was, but had a huge estate in Yorkshire, besides a house in London and another at Newmarket where he trained his race-horses."

Noella had listened enthralled.

"He was a strange man," Mrs. Wakefield said, "and I thought when I met him rather frightening."

"You met him, Mama?"

"Of course I met him," her mother replied, "first when Caroline became engaged to him and he came to stay with her parents, and then soon after she was married I visited Caroline in Yorkshire."

"Tell me about it, Mama!"

Mrs. Wakefield hesitated a moment before she said;

"I think it was then I realised for the first time that Caroline's husband was nearly old enough to be her father!"

She paused before she went on:

"He was handsome, at the same time very authoritative, and I thought he treated Caroline rather as if she was a School-girl."

"Did she mind that, Mama?" Noella enquired.

"She did not say very much," Mrs. Wakefield replied, "but I thought she seemed a little restless, and not as happy as I would have wanted her to be."

She sighed and continued:

"As Yorkshire is so far away, that was the only time I stayed with her there, although I was their guest on several occasions after the Earl opened Raven House in London. Caroline and I had a marvellous time attending Balls and of course shopping."

Mrs. Wakefield's eyes were very tender as she said:

"Caroline loved me and we were in fact like sisters. She shared her clothes with me, just as when we were children we shared our toys."

"It must have been wonderful for you, Mama!" Noella exclaimed.

"It was indeed," Mrs. Wakefield agreed. "For the first time in my life I wore expensive and very beautiful gowns and, without being conceited, I can tell you, Dearest, I was a social success!"

"How could you be anything else, Mama, when you are so beautiful?"

"Not as beautiful as Caroline, but when your father saw me for the first time at a Ball given at Raven House, he said he knew I was the girl he wanted to marry."

"That was romantic, Mama!" Noella exclaimed.

"It was the most glorious thing that ever happened to me," Mrs. Wakefield replied, "and I wish I could describe to you how handsome your father looked in his uniform!"

"So you fell in love with him, Mama?"

"How could I do anything else?" Mrs. Wakefield answered. "Unfortunately, however, it was impossible for us to be married as soon as we would have liked because he was leaving almost immediately with a Battalion of his Regiment for India."

Noella gave a little cry.

"Oh, Mama, that must have been heart-breaking for you both."

"He just had time to tell me how much he loved me," Mrs. Wakefield said, "and asked me to wait for him, which I promised to do."

"Then he was . . gone," Noella murmured.

"I went back to the country after he had left," Mrs. Wakefield related, "and knew that no other man had ever seemed so attractive or meant so much to me."

"But I am sure there were other men who wanted to marry you," Noella suggested.

"There were two or three," Mrs. Wakefield admitted, "and there would have been more if I had encouraged them."

"But you had to wait a long time for Papa."

"Nearly eight years," Mrs. Wakefield said, "and when he did come home, I was desperately afraid that he would no longer wish to marry me."

"He had written to you."

"He wrote to me two or three times a week," Mrs.

Wakefield said proudly, "telling me I was always in his thoughts, and that he was praying that his Regiment would soon be sent home."

"Did you never think of going to India to join him?" Noella asked.

"It was a journey which took nearly six months," Mrs. Wakefield explained, "and even if my father and mother could have afforded it, they would not have wanted me to travel so far from home."

"Oh, poor Mama! So you had to wait all that time!" Noella cried.

"In a way I was quite happy, and when finally your father returned, we were married immediately even though he had been wounded and the doctors advised him to rest."

Mrs. Wakefield gave a little laugh as she went on:

"But you know what your father was like when he made up his mind to do something! As he was determined to marry me and all the doctors in the world could not have prevented his doing so. We were married in the village Church with only a few friends to drink our health."

"You must have felt it was very unlike the grand wedding your Cousin Caroline had," Noella said reflectively.

"Caroline's wedding was sensational and she had seven other bridesmaids beside myself."

Mrs. Wakefield's eyes were dreamy as she went on:

"I had no bridesmaids and no pages, but I felt as I married your father that the angels were singing overhead and we were enveloped by a Divine Light."

There was a little tremor in her voice as she went on:

"Three months later I found I was having a baby, and that was you, my darling."

"Were you excited, Mama?"

"I was so thrilled and excited, and so was your father, that we thought no two people in the world could be as happy as we were."

"And you told your Cousin Caroline," Noella prompted knowing what came next.

14

"Yes, I wrote to Caroline," Mrs. Wakefield agreed, "and she wrote back saying that by a strange coincidence she was having another baby. She already had a son who was born nine months after she was married."

Looking back into the past Mrs. Wakefield went on to describe how she and her Cousin Caroline had written to each other every week.

They described how they were feeling and what they were thinking.

Then a strange thing happened:

Their letters crossed, and as the Countess of Ravensdale opened hers in Yorkshire, Mrs. Wakefield was opening hers in Worcestershire.

They found they had both written the same thing to each other.

"My baby will be born, the Doctors think, either on, or around Christmas Day, and I am sure, dearest, it will be the same for you. I suggest therefore that if it is a boy, we call him Noel, and if it is a girl, Noella."

"It was not really so extraordinary that we each had had the same idea and had written to the other to say so," Mrs. Wakefield said to her daughter, "because Caroline and I have always been so close to each other."

She smiled as she added:

"We not only thought alike, but we were alike in looks, and I think we both expected that our babies also would look alike, although they had different fathers."

Noella as she grew up had always been intensely curious about Noella Raven, who like herself had been born on Christmas Day, but they had never met.

She did not understand the reason for this.

Eventually however, her mother explained in a low, rather shocked voice what had happened.

Two years after the Countess of Ravensdale had produced her daughter she had fallen wildly and crazily in love.

She and her husband had met him at Newmarket while attending a race meeting.

Captain D'Arcy Fairburn was a dashing, handsome Rake who had left behind him a trail of broken hearts wherever he went.

Yet he had so much charm that it would have been impossible for him not to be liked and accepted by the men as well as women in the Social World.

He came of a good family, but he was a gambler.

Most of his more Puritanical relations looked down their noses when his name was mentioned.

This did not disturb D'Arcy Fairburn in the slightest, as he flitted from *Boudoir* to *Boudoir*.

At the same time, because he was a good sportsman, he was accepted by the Jockey Club and by the members of all the most exclusive Clubs in St. James's.

It was only to be expected, because he was a 'Pied Piper' where women were concerned, that Caroline, after spending the last two years almost exclusively in Yorkshire, would fall in love with him.

What was surprising was that he lost his heart completely to her.

"It was a horrifying surprise to me as it must have been to many other people," Mrs. Wakefield said in a low voice, "when Caroline ran away with Captain D'Arcy Fairburn, taking her daughter Noella with her."

"But surely, Mama, people were very shocked?" Noella exclaimed.

"Of course they were," her mother replied, "and the Earl was very angry – very angry indeed!"

"What happened?" Noella enquired.

"Caroline wrote to tell me that she was going abroad. They went first to Paris, then travelled to many places in Europe where Captain Fairburn could gamble."

"Why did the Earl not divorce her?" Noella had asked.

"It was what everybody expected him to do," her mother replied, "but he was very proud, and would not face the scandal it would entail if he took his case to the House of Lords."

"What happened then?"

"Caroline disappeared and I did not hear from her for several years."

Mrs. Wakefield's voice told Noella how much she had minded. But she went on:

"Then she wrote to me one Christmas, telling me how pretty her daughter was and wondering if she looked like you."

"Which of course she did!" Noella exclaimed.

She was only aware of this later.

At the time, she had listened while her mother explained that her Cousin Caroline had given up her title and called herself "Mrs. Fairburn".

"She hoped," Mrs. Wakefield explained, "that most people she met abroad would not be aware that the man she was with was not in reality her husband."

"What happened," Noella asked, "to the son that Cousin Caroline left behind?"

"She left him with his father because of course, he was the heir to the Earldom. I have often wondered," Mrs. Wakefield sighed, "if he was lonely and unhappy without his mother."

It had all seemed a fascinating story, but rather complicated.

Noella did not think about it very much however, until a year ago quite unexpectedly Mrs. Fairburn, as she called herself, and her daughter Noella arrived at their house.

It was early one evening and Noella was sitting with her mother in front of the fire in the Sitting-Room.

They were wondering how they could alter a gown to make it look more fashionable when there was a knock on the front door.

"I wonder who that can be?" Mrs. Wakefield exclaimed.

"I will answer it, Mama," Noella replied. "Nanny is busy preparing supper in the kitchen."

She had hurried from the small Sitting-Room across the narrow hall and opened the front door.

To her astonishment there was a carriage outside.

Standing on the doorstep was a Lady, muffled up against the cold, and with her a young girl.

For a moment she just stared at them. Then the Lady said:

"You must be Noella!"

At that moment Mrs. Wakefield had come out into the hall and she gave a cry of sheer astonishment.

"Caroline! Can it really be you?"

"It is, and Oh, Averil, I have come to you for help!'

The two women kissed while Noella stared in astonishment at her namesake.

There was no doubt that she might have been looking at a picture of herself.

Noella, whom she was to learn her mother always called Noely, had the same fair hair, the same dark blue eyes and a smile that was curiously like her own.

"We might be twins!" Noely said.

Then as Mrs. Wakefield drew them towards the fire the driver of the hired carriage began to bring in their trunks.

Their story took some time to tell and it was a very sad one.

Captain D'Arcy Fairburn had grown even more reckless in his gambling as he grew older.

Although Mrs. Fairburn spoke about it in a whisper to her cousin, Noella overheard what she said.

He had been obliged to obtain money in a somewhat reprehensible manner from women to pay his bills.

Then there was a furious row which took place at a card-game when he had been challenged to a duel.

His wife had been frantic with anxiety.

She had however laughed away her fears, knowing he had fought many duels at one time or another, so one more was really of little consequence.

Now however, he was older than he had been in the past, and because his opponent was not only younger but also a better shot, Captain Fairburn died three days after the duel had taken place.

Caroline and Noely had found themselves practically penniless.

"I thought I had many friends in Naples, which is where we were at the time," Caroline said, "but they drifted away like the mist. I realised then that the only thing for Noely and me was to come back to England."

"That was sensible of you," Mrs. Wakefield approved.

"We have no money," Caroline went on, "and I do not know where to turn to get any."

"But of course you can stay here," Mrs. Wakefield said warmly.

"Dearest Averil, I knew you would say that , but I hate to impose on you."

"You are not imposing, and it will be wonderful for me to be with you again."

Cousin Caroline's companionship had certainly, Noella thought, made her mother very happy and she too had enjoyed being with Noely.

They might look alike but actually Noely, having lived on the Continent, seemed older.

She had met a large number of people and travelled from one gambling Casino to another.

She talked of things that Noella had never heard of, and she had in some ways, a cynical regard for the world.

It certainly belied the beauty of her face.

"Papa was hopeless about money," she said to Noella.

She had already learnt that Noely called Captain Fairburn 'Papa', even though he was not her real father.

"It must have been .. very difficult for you," Noella said hesitatingly.

"At times it was hell!" Noely replied. "We often had to sponge on strangers for our meals, or else go hungry!"

There was a sharp note in her voice that Noella did not miss.

When they got to know each other better, Noely confided in her one evening:

"I got so tired of wondering where our next meal was coming from, that when we were in Venice I sat down and

19

wrote to my real father the Earl of Ravensdale."

Noella gave a little gasp.

"That was very brave of you!"

"I told him how miserable I was, traipsing about Europe wherever there was a Casino and asked him if I could come home."

Noella gave another gasp.

Her first thought was that it was very disloyal of Noely to do such a thing behind her Mother's back.

Then she understood how difficult it was for them always being without money and also how humiliating for Noely to have to pretend to be the daughter of a man who was not able to marry her mother.

"I suppose you realise," Noely went on, "that if I could be my real self, I am Lady Noella Raven!"

"I never thought of it," Noella exclaimed.

"Well, it is true, but of course I realise now that D'Arcy Fairburn is dead, that I have to look after Mama."

She sighed.

"As it is obvious my father will never forgive her for running away, and her own relations will not speak to her either, I have no choice but to exist as I am."

"Oh, Noely, I am so sorry," Noella said, "but perhaps something will turn up."

"What?" Noely asked.

As it happened, what did turn up was not only unexpected, but also a tragedy.

They struggled along for some months, living very frugally on Mrs. Wakefield's small pension, and talking incessantly of how they could make money.

Mrs. Wakefield learnt that Caroline had sold her furs and everything else she possessed of any value to pay the fares which brought them back to England.

She had, in fact, when she arrived only a few pounds to her name.

They were all four aware that the way they were living could not go on for ever.

One morning there was a letter for Mrs. Fairburn and

when she opened it, she gave a cry of sheer joy.

"This is good news!" she exclaimed. "Wonderful news, Averil! You will be as excited as I am!"

"What has happened?" Mrs. Wakefield asked.

"A friend, a very kind friend, Mr. Leon Rothman, is arriving in England tomorrow, and wishes to see me at once!"

She looked at Noely and went on:

"Do you remember, Dearest, when we left Italy I left a note at his Villa to say that you and I were coming to England and would, we hoped, be staying here."

There was a note in her voice that had not been there before as she explained to Mrs. Wakefield:

"He was in Africa at the time, so he did not receive my letter until he returned to Naples a week ago. Now he has come speeding after me, and everything will be different!"

"Are you telling me, Caroline," Mrs. Wakefield said softly, "that you are going to marry this gentleman?"

Caroline looked at her in surprise. Then she said:

"Marry him? But that is impossible! He is married already! But he is rich, very, very rich, and he has always been a very devoted . . friend."

There was a pause before the word '*friend*' that said a great deal more than Caroline had put into words.

Noella did not understand, but her mother did and there was an expression of disapproval in Mrs. Wakefield's eyes as she rose from the table.

"I hope, Caroline dear, that you will not be disappointed," she said after a moment and went from the room.

Caroline and Noely had set off the next morning, hiring a Post Chaise to take them to Worcester where Mr. Rothman had said he would be staying at the best Hotel and would be waiting to greet them.

"I am sure he will want us to go to London with him immediately," Caroline said confidently, "and we will send for the rest of our luggage, although I expect he will buy us anything we require."

She and Noely took with them enough for two or three nights.

They were both so excited as they drove away that it took Noella a little time to realise how much her mother disapproved of what was happening.

They had gone back into the Sitting-Room and Mrs. Wakefield had said unexpectedly:

"Oh, my Dearest, if only you had the chance of meeting the sort of people I knew when I was young, it would make me so happy!"

"What sort of people?" Noella asked.

"Ladies and Gentlemen who live respectable lives!" Mrs. Wakefield replied sharply.

She had taken her daughter by the hand and drawn her down on the sofa beside her.

"Listen, Noella," she said, "you are nearly eighteen and you are intelligent enough to realise that some people do strange and perhaps wrong things in their lives. But that is their concern! Promise me you will always try to do what is right and good."

"But, of course, Mama!"

Her mother had spoken so earnestly that after a moment Noella said;

"It is your Cousin Caroline who is upsetting you, Mama, is it not? But why? Do you think it wrong of her to be so excited at seeing this gentleman?"

She thought for a moment that her mother was not going to reply.

Then she said;

"I love Caroline, as I have ever since we were children together, but you, Dearest, have to understand that it was wrong of her to leave her husband and go away with a man she could not marry."

She paused obviously feeling for words and went on;

"It is also wrong for her to meet this Mr. Rothman, whoever he may be, and expect him to look after her when he has a wife and family of his own."

"I understand, Mama, what you are saying," Noella said after a moment.

"Love is a very strange thing," her mother continued.

"One day you will understand that when one is in love everything seems a little out of perspective and nothing may seem to matter except the wonder and glory of it."

She drew in her breath before she went on quietly;

"But love is given to us by God, and if we abuse it, if we do what is wrong, then we are desecrating something which is perfect and is, in fact, Divine."

Noella looked surprised and her mother bent forward to kiss her.

"I am praying with all my heart," she said, "that one day you will find a man as fine and as noble as your father with whom you will fall in love. Then you will understand that any love that breaks God's rules spoils and defiles those who accept it."

Mrs. Wakefield had risen from the sofa as she finished speaking, walking out of the room so that her daughter should not see her tears.

After she had gone Noella puzzled over what she had said.

She could not help thinking it was very sad that Noely should be so poor and could have none of the things to which she was entitled as her father's daughter.

"Perhaps one day he will forgive Cousin Caroline," Noella told herself optimistically "then Noely can be herself and live in the luxury she longs for."

Because she herself had never known luxury, Noella did not miss it.

But she did not know at the time what disaster was awaiting her, or how Fate was going to change her life.

Three days after they had left Cousin Caroline and Noely returned.

As soon as Noella had run to the door to greet them she realised that something terrible had happened.

They came into the house, white-faced and obviously very perturbed and as Caroline sat down in the Sitting-Room as if her legs would no longer support her, she said to Mrs. Wakefield;

"I can hardly bear to tell you – I can hardly believe it myself! But Leon Rothman is dead!"

"Dead?" Mrs. Wakefield ejaculated.

"He died early this morning and Noely and I left at once!"

"But – why? What happened?"

"He contracted a fever in Africa and should have gone to Hospital when he returned to Naples. But when he had read my letter he was determined to come here to help me, as I had begged him to do."

Caroline Fairburn's voice broke before with an effort she went on:

"The journey to England made his fever grow worse, and there was underlying it some insidious poison that spread through his whole body."

With a sob she continued:

"When we arrived at the hotel his manservant told me how ill he was, and although they had sent for a doctor in the town, he had no idea how to treat him."

There were tears in Caroline's eyes as she went on:

"He fought against it, he fought for life with the same determination he had shown in his business deals. But he died! We came away feeling we had failed him, but it was impossible to help a man who was no .. longer with .. us."

Caroline burst into tears and Mrs. Wakefield put her arms around her.

"I am sorry. I am so sorry!" she murmured.

"Oh, Averil, what am I to do? He was my last hope, and now the sooner I die, the better!"

Mrs. Wakefield tried to comfort her, then because she knew she was exhausted, persuaded her to go to bed.

The next morning, Noella awoke to the horror that both Caroline and her daughter had contracted the fever that had killed Leon Rothman.

The local doctor was called but could suggest nothing except that they stay in bed.

He prescribed some medicine which Mrs. Wakefield thought was little more than coloured water.

She firmly refused to allow Noella to go near either Noely or her mother, insisting that Mrs. Wakefield alone should nurse them.

Noella protested, but her mother would not listen.

"You are to keep out of their rooms, my dearest," she said to her daughter. "You can help Nanny in the kitchen and bring the food upstairs, but if you go near either of them I shall be very, very angry!"

"You know I will do what you say, Mama," Noella replied, "but do not overtire yourself."

Afterwards she thought it was because her mother did tire herself and was already not in particularly good health that she in her turn contracted the fever.

Caroline and her daughter died within a few hours of each other, and before their bodies could be taken from the house, her mother also was dead.

At first Noella thought it was just a nightmare from which she could not awaken.

When the Funerals were over she and Nanny were left alone in the quiet, empty house with no money.

They found that day by day it was growing more and more difficult to live.

Chapter Two

"I must have some money!" Noella said to herself.

She wondered if she should look round the rest of the house.

It was quite useless for her to do so because already she had sold everything she could from her mother's bedroom, and the other rooms as well.

It was Nanny who had said there was no point in keeping her Cousin Caroline and Noely's clothes.

Noella had hesitated however before she had agreed.

"Perhaps they are . . infectious," she suggested.

"We've taken care of the rooms," Nanny said, "but to make sure, I'll put them outside in the air."

It was the doctor who had said firmly that the rooms in which Cousin Caroline and Noely had died had to be fumigated.

They were shut up and an evil-smelling disinfectant was burned in them.

The smell of it permeated the whole house.

Only by opening all the windows and doors, and in fact, keeping outside as much as possible, did Noella gradually escape from what she felt was the smell of death.

Nanny had taken out the clothes which had belonged to Cousin Caroline and Noella had hung them on the line in the garden.

After they had stayed there for nearly three days, Noella felt they could no longer be infectious.

She had sold them for a few shillings to the Carrier who came through the village once a week.

He was always prepared to buy anything on which he made a profit on his rounds.

Noella did however have to keep the evening-gowns which were far too elaborate and too décolleté to be worn by any respectable English girl.

They were therefore left hanging in the room that Cousin Caroline had used.

The Carrier had also taken the last remaining garments which had belonged to Mrs. Wakefield.

It hurt Noella to dispose of them, but she felt at the moment it was more important to eat than to be clothed.

She had not only herself to think of, but there was Nanny who was nearly sixty and had been with her ever since she had been a baby.

There was also Hawkins, who had been her father's Batman and had left the Regiment when he retired.

He had been employed ostensibly to groom his horses but he soon became a general factotum ready to do anything that was required of him.

She often thought it was due to Hawkins that she and Nanny were still alive.

In the last month they had relied on the rabbits he had snared in the wood beyond the garden and the fish, tiny though they were, which he caught in the stream.

Up to Christmas they had been able to keep going with the potatoes he had grown and stored away in an old shed.

By the New Year, however, they were desperate.

There were days when they had to subsist on the stale bread which the Baker let them have for a penny or two because it was no longer saleable

Hawkins was not as young as he was; in fact he was getting on for seventy.

Noella knew he was looking older than his years because he was underfed.

The same applied to Nanny.

Although they never said so, Noella knew at the back of her mind that they were terrified in case they should end up in the Workhouse.

'I have to save them, even if I cannot save myself,' she thought, but had no idea how she could do it.

She had of course, thought of selling the house but because it was so dilapidated and in such an isolated part of the country there were no purchasers.

She sometimes thought the roof would fall down on them and become their tombstone.

"I have to do something!" she said aloud, walking across to the window.

Then because she was frightened she began to pray not only to God, but also to her mother.

She was startled by a sharp knock on the front door.

She knew it was unlikely that Nanny would hear it, so she turned from the window and went to answer it.

She had the uncomfortable feeling it might be somebody from the village asking her to pay a bill, and she knew how embarrassing it would be to explain that she literally had no money with which to do so.

Tentatively, because she was nervous, she opened the door.

Then to her astonishment she saw outside a very elegant Gentleman dressed in the height of fashion.

There stood outside, in which obviously he had arrived, a Travelling Chariot, drawn by two well-bred horses.

There was a groom standing at their heads, and a Coachman on the box.

As she looked first at the Gentleman, then at the horses and back again he said;

"I wish to speak to Lady Noella Raven!"

Noella started with surprise, then before she could reply the Gentleman said;

"In fact I think you must be Lady Noella! I am your Cousin – Jasper Raven!"

He swept his hat from his head as he spoke and Noella said hastily;

"No, no, I am not Lady Noella, but perhaps you should come in so that I can explain."

"Certainly," the Gentleman agreed.

28

He entered the hall and Noella knew he was looking around to find somewhere to put his hat.

She had sold the table and the two rather attractive oak chairs and had forgotten that the hall would surprisingly seem empty to a stranger.

She said nothing but led the way into the Sitting-Room and saw the Gentleman raise his eye-brows when he was aware of how little furniture it contained.

He however, waited for Noella to suggest that he sat down.

Then he rather gingerly lowered himself into one of the arm-chairs and set his hat down on the floor beside him.

Noella seated herself on the sofa and said;

"I am afraid, Mr. Raven, I have . . bad news for you!"

"Bad news?" Jasper Raven repeated, and his voice was sharp.

"Lady Noella and her mother . . are dead."

"Dead? I do not believe you!" Mr. Raven exclaimed.

"I am afraid it is true," Noella said. "They contracted an African fever from a friend who had just arrived in England and there was nothing the doctor or my mother could do to save them."

He did not speak and she added:

"M . . my mother . . caught the fever from them and . . she died too!"

"I am sorry," Mr. Raven said. "It must have been a great shock."

"I still find it hard to believe it had really happened."

As Noella spoke she realised that her visitor was frowning.

When she looked at him more closely she saw that he was not as young as she had at first thought when she saw him on the door-step.

She guessed that he was perhaps thirty-five and although he was tall and slender, he was not good-looking.

There was something rather hard about his face.

Then, because she could not help being curious, she remarked:

"You said you were a relative of Noella's?"

"As I have already told you, my name is Raven," the Gentleman replied, "and I am a cousin of the Earl of Ravensdale."

"Noely had been hoping to hear from her father," Noella began.

"That is impossible – he is dead!"

"Oh . .! She told me she had written to him when she and her mother were in Venice, but it never struck her that that was the reason why he did not reply to her letter."

"There was no reply for the simple reason that the Earl was very ill. It was only when his son returned from abroad after his death that his correspondence was dealt with."

"I wish Noely had known that," Noella said to herself.

"Well, it is too late now," Mr. Raven remarked somewhat unsympathetically, "and my journey round Europe has been a waste of time!"

He spoke in a tone that seemed to Noella to be more bitter than sad.

She could only say softly:

"I am so sorry, and I think Noely, if she were alive, would have been very thrilled to meet one of her Raven relatives."

"But that does not help me!" the Gentleman said.

Noella looked puzzled, and as if he felt he must talk to somebody he explained:

"Lady Noella's death is a disaster as far as I personally am concerned."

"But, why?" Noella asked.

"Her brother, now the Earl, sent me to find her, and informed me it would be to my advantage if I did so. He wanted her to come to live with him."

"I wish she had known," Noella said regretfully.

Then because she was interested she asked:

"What is the Earl like? Cousin Caroline never spoke of him."

"*Cousin* Caroline?" Mr. Raven repeated. "Are you telling me that you are a relation of the family?"

"Not of the Ravens," Noella answered, "but Noella's mother, whom I suppose I should refer to as The Countess, was my mother's cousin, and her greatest friend."

She saw Mr. Raven was interested and went on:

"When Captain D'Arcy Fairburn died, Cousin Caroline and Noely came back to England to stay with us. They were however very poor and it would have been wonderful if the Earl could have assisted his sister in some way."

"That is what he intended to do," Mr. Raven said, "and he also promised to assist me if I could find her."

"You do not look as though you needed any assistance," Noella said without thinking.

Mr. Raven laughed.

"Appearances can be deceptive, and I assure you, I am very much in need of money."

Then in a change of tone he said:

"I fear it is very remiss of me, but I have not yet asked you your name."

Noella smiled.

"It may surprise you to hear that I also am Noella. When my mother and Cousin Caroline knew their babies were to be born at Christmas they agreed that they should both have the same name: Noel if a boy, and Noella if a girl."

"I should have thought that might prove rather complicated," Mr. Raven remarked.

"It might have been, if we had always been together," Noella agreed. "But actually I had never met Noely until she arrived here last year, and it was very strange to find that we looked so much like each other."

"Of course!" Mr. Raven said, as if he had just thought of it. "Her hair was the same colour as yours!"

Noella smiled as she explained:

"My mother always said it was some Swedish ancestor, far back in history, who was responsible for our hair and it recurs from time to time in the family."

As she spoke she was aware that Mr. Raven was looking at her in a scrutinising manner which made her feel a little uncomfortable.

Then he felt in the pocket of his tight-fitting coat and brought out a small leather case.

He opened it, and revealed that inside there was a miniature portrait.

He handed it to Noella who saw it depicted Noely when she was very young, in fact not much more than a year old.

But her pale gold hair was unmistakable, so were her dark blue eyes.

"That is almost exactly how Noely looked when she was grown up!" she exclaimed in delight.

"It could also quite easily be you!" Mr. Raven remarked.

Noella smiled at him and handed him back the miniature.

Then she said:

"I feel embarrassed that I cannot . . offer you any refreshment, but I am . . afraid there is . . nothing in the . house."

There was a little pause before he asked:

"Why are you so poor?"

Noella made a helpless little gesture with her hands.

"My father's pension died with my mother," she said, "and as you can see, there is nothing . . else to . . sell."

She spoke simply and somehow, because it was so obvious, it was not even embarrassing.

It flashed through her mind that if Noely had received help from her brother, she would have been able to help her too. She was quite certain she would have wanted to.

Unexpectedly Mr. Raven walked across the room to stand looking at the untidy garden.

"Who is here with you?" he asked without turning round.

"My old Nanny, and my father's soldier servant, who has been here since Papa retired and bought the house."

"Surely you have friends in the neighbourhood?" he asked.

"There are very few people round here, and most of them are not well off themselves."

As she spoke Noella thought how embarrassing it would be to have to beg from her neighbours.

They had paid very little attention to her since her mother's death.

They were mostly old, and their families, if they had any, had moved to London or to other parts of the country, which were more interesting than this isolated part of Worcestershire.

They certainly had not sent her many invitations, and she had been too shy, or too proud, to deliberately seek them out and plead for help.

Mr. Raven turned round from the window and walked back to the chair in which he had been sitting and sat down again.

"You have not yet told me your surname," he said.

"I am sorry, I should have done so when you first arrived. My name is Noella Wakefield."

"Listen to me, Miss Wakefield," Mr. Raven said, "because I think it might be to your advantage."

He spoke slowly, as if he was choosing his words and thinking over what he should say.

Noella looked at him wide-eyed.

She had the feeling that what he was going to say to her was important, but she could not imagine what it could be.

"Two months ago," Mr. Raven began, "I went to see my cousin, the Earl of Ravensdale, with the plans of an invention which I thought might interest him."

"An invention!" Noella exclaimed.

"A new telescope which is more advanced than anything that is being used by the Navy at present, and which

I am convinced will be a successful money-maker if it is put on the market."

"How interesting!" Noella agreed.

"I asked my Cousin Lyndon if he would finance my venture," Mr. Raven went on, "but, needless to say, he was not particularly enthusiastic."

"Why not?" Noella asked.

"Because he is hard and difficult as his father was before him!" Mr. Raven said sharply.

"Mama thought that Cousin Caroline's husband was very autocratic and rather frightening!" Noella said. "It seems sad that Noely's brother should be the same."

"Many people find him intimidating," Mr. Raven said. "I merely find him ungenerous."

"Because he refused to finance your invention?"

"I have a friend who is an expert in these things," Mr. Raven replied, "and he is convinced it is really revolutionary and very far in advance of what is being used at the moment."

Noella wondered how this concerned Noely.

Then as if he could read her thoughts Mr. Raven said;

"After a great deal of argument the Earl said that if I could produce a telescope that could see further than ever before, I should be able to find his sister whom he had not heard of until he read the letter she had written to his father."

"Oh! Now I understand!" Noella exclaimed, "and it was very clever of you to trace Noely here."

"I first went to Venice from where her letter had been written," Mr. Raven said, "and after tracing innumerable people who had known Captain Fairburn when he was there, I followed their trail to Naples."

"It was from Naples that Cousin Caroline and Noely came here," Noella remarked.

"That is what I understood," Mr. Raven said, "but now that I have arrived, I find my journey has been wasted!"

"I am sorry, so very sorry," Noella cried, "but unfortunately there is nothing we can do about it."

"In fact, I think there is!" Mr. Raven said quietly.

Noella looked at him in surprise and he said:

"You tell me you are in looks very like your cousin."

"So alike," Noella replied, "that we might be identical twins!"

Mr. Raven bent forward in his chair.

"I have a proposition to put to you."

"A .. proposition?"

"I have the idea, Miss Wakefield, that you are desperately in need of money."

"I should have .. thought that was very .. obvious," Noella replied, "and as you can see .. I have nothing .. left to .. sell."

"I am aware of that, and also that you are far thinner than you should be."

Mr. Raven's eyes flickered over her and Noella felt herself blushing.

Because she thought he was being slightly impertinent she said:

"I expect we shall manage, and I am only sorry, Mr. Raven, that your journey has been so unfruitful."

She rose to her feet, but to her surprise he made no effort to move.

He merely looked up at her with the sunshine glinting on her hair.

It made it seem as if it was a halo of light round her thin, pointed face.

"Sit down!" he said sharply.

Noella was so surprised that she obeyed him.

"Now listen to me," he said, "and try to understand what I am saying."

Noella just looked at him and he went on:

"The Earl of Ravensdale has made up his mind that he wishes to take his sister away from the life which he believes she is living with her mother and Captain D'Arcy Fairburn."

Noella was listening with a somewhat puzzled expression in her eyes.

"I promised to find this young woman for the Earl, but alas she is no longer on this earth. I think, however, the gods have been kind and have sent a substitute."

He twisted his lips as he spoke.

Then as he realised that Noella had not followed him, he said:

"What I am suggesting is that you take your cousin's place!"

Noella stared at him.

"I . . I do not . . understand!"

"I think you now do," Mr. Raven corrected. "You have seen the miniature, and you must know that no one could deny that you are the child it portrays."

"Wh . . what are you . . saying?" Noella asked.

"Try to understand," Mr. Raven said sharply. "The Earl of Ravensdale wants his sister. I can either return to tell him she is dead and there is no chance of his being able to see her."

He paused to smile, before he continued:

"Or I can take back with me somebody who resembles her so closely that, as you have said yourself, you might have been twins!"

"Are you suggesting that I should . . pretend to be . . Noely?" Noella gasped.

"I am not only suggesting it," Mr. Raven said, "I am telling you that you will be an extremely foolish young woman if you do not agree!"

"No . . of course not . . how could I . . do such a thing?" Noella exclaimed.

Mr. Raven got to his feet.

"In which case my journey has been wasted and I can only hope, Miss Wakefield, that you will enjoy starving yourself to death as you are apparently doing at the moment."

Mr. Raven bent to pick up his hat, then he walked towards the door.

Only as he reached it did Noella say as if she spoke to herself:

"How could I .. possibly do such a thing? It would be deceitful and .. wrong."

"Wrong for whom?" Mr. Raven asked. "For yourself? For your servants who I imagine look as thin and as hungry as you do?"

It was when he spoke of the servants that it flashed through Noella's mind that she could not deliberately let Nanny and Hawkins starve.

Certainly not, if there was any alternative.

Only this morning as Nanny toasted her some of the stale bread for breakfast and added a tiny portion of the fish which Hawkins had caught yesterday, she had said:

"That's all there is, an' if you're thanking God for small mercies, you might point out to Him that they're very small indeed!"

Noella looked down at the food on her plate and Nanny had added:

"There's nothing to drink except water. We finished up the tea two days ago, an' I thinks I'd rather be in my grave than without a cup o' tea for breakfast!"

She had walked out of the room before Noella could reply.

She had known that to be without her tea was to Nanny the worst privation of all.

She was sure Hawkins felt the same as Nanny.

When having eaten the minute portion of fish on the toast on which there was no butter, she told herself they could not go on like this.

If they did, they would, in Nanny's words, "soon be in their graves".

Now as she stared at Mr. Raven she was thinking that if she did as he suggested, she would be rescuing not only herself, but also Nanny and Hawkins.

She had lain awake half the previous night, thinking about them.

They had been so loyal and neither of them ever complained that they had received no wages since her mother had died.

In their usual philosophical manner, they had been sure that something would 'turn up' although they had no idea what it could possibly be.

Here was the answer, and in a voice that trembled, Noella said pleadingly:

"Could you .. explain a little more .. clearly what .. you want me .. to do?"

There was a faint smile on Jasper Raven's face as he walked slowly back to the chair and sat down.

"What happpened is quite simple," he said in a low voice. "This fever which you have been talking about killed Caroline, the Countess of Ravensdale and her great friend with whom she was staying, Mrs. Wakefield."

He paused for a moment before he said:

"When I arrived, you were wondering desperately what you should do about yourself."

"But surely .. if I am .. pretending to be Noely .. the Earl will be .. suspicious?"

"Why should he be?" Mr. Raven enquired. "He has not seen his sister since she was two years old, and when his mother ran away he was only eleven."

"But .." Noella began.

"There are no 'buts' about it," Mr. Raven interrupted. "You will not be expected to know any more about the family than you know at the moment, since your mother would not talk about her life before she decided to live with D'Arcy Fairburn in what your relatives call 'sin'!"

"I can understand their .. being very .. shocked," Noella murmured.

She remembered what she had felt when her mother first told her about Caroline's behaviour.

"It is something they are not likely to discuss with you," Mr. Raven said. "Now I suggest that we leave here as quickly as possible and start our journey to Yorkshire where your 'brother' is waiting for you."

Noella gave a little cry.

"But .. I cannot go .. just like .. that!"

"Why not?" he asked. "I cannot believe you are leaving

much of any importance behind you here."

Noella looked around her in a dazed fashion. Then she said:

"You understand that I have to take .. Nanny and Hawkins with .. me?"

"Good Heavens, that is quite unnecessary!" Mr. Raven said. "I will give them some money and they can find themselves other positions."

"No .. no! Of course not!" Noella exclaimed. "They must come with me .. or I will not .. go!"

"It is impossible," he said, "because they will then have to be let into the secret."

"I would trust both of them with my life!"

She saw he was going to be difficult and added:

"Nanny came to look after me when I was born, and Hawkins was with Papa in his Regiment."

She gave a little cry before she said:

"They have been so loyal .. so wonderful to me! Either they .. come with me .. or else I must .. stay here!"

She spoke so firmly that she knew Mr. Raven was impressed.

Once again he rose to walk across the room and look out of the window as if he was trying to think things over in his mind.

Then he said:

"Very well, have it your own way! But if they expose you and the Earl throws you out into the gutter, then it is entirely your own fault!"

Noella knew she had won and she said:

"May I suggest that as we cannot give you any luncheon here, you go to the Posting House which is two or three miles up the road? When you return we shall have packed up all we have to take with us."

"A Posting House? We shall need that!"

He thought Noella looked surprised and he said:

"You can hardly expect me to accommodate so many people together with your luggage, in my chariot."

Because Noella had the feeling that perhaps he was

trying to separate her from Nanny and Hawkins she said:

"I do not see why not! Hawkins can sit on the box with your coachman and Nanny can face us on the small seat. What little luggage we have can be tied on behind."

Mr. Raven thought this over, then he said:

"I have borrowed my Travelling Chariot from a friend. We shall need something larger and more comfortable in which to travel to Yorkshire."

He sounded so reluctant to do what she asked that Noella said:

"Are you .. quite certain you are .. wise to do this? Would it not be better if you .. went away and .. forgot about me?"

"What, and lose my chance of your so-called brother financing my telescope? No, Lady Noella, you can travel as you wish, and I will make the best of it."

Noella did not miss the way he addressed her.

A few minutes later as she showed him out through the front door she could hardly believe that the whole thing was not a hoax.

She felt that having left, he would never return.

Then because she realised that if he did come back there was very little time, she ran to the kitchen.

Nanny was cooking something on the stove and Hawkins had just come in carrying a pile of logs for the fire.

The one thing of which there was plenty was wood and at least they had not been cold in the house all during the winter.

The trees were thick in the copse which bordered the garden, and however hungry they might be there had always been big log fires to keep them warm.

Nanny could also cook on them, when there was anything to cook.

Now Noella sat down at the kitchen-table and told Nanny and Hawkins to listen to her.

She was sure they would think the whole thing was part of her imagination, or else she had been asleep and dreaming.

They stared at her at first incredulously.

Then as she told them exactly what Mr. Raven had proposed, Nanny exclaimed;

"Your dear mother, God rest her soul, would turn over in her grave, that she would, at the very idea of your acting a lie!"

"I know, Nanny. I thought that myself, but I cannot believe Mama would wish us to stay here without food, and starve to death!"

She looked at Hawkins as if for support, and she thought there was a twinkle in his eyes as he said:

"If yer asks me, wot Miss Noella's suggestin' won't 'urt no-one. An' it'll be a treat to 'ave our bellies full for a change!"

"Right is right, and wrong is wrong, Mr. Hawkins!" Nanny said tartly.

"An' it ain't right," Mr. Hawkins replied, "to see Miss Noella gettin' thinner every day, until a puff of wind'll blow 'er away!"

Nanny looked at Noella in silence.

They were both aware that she had had to take in Noella's dresses round the waist almost every week. Even so, they still hung loosely on her.

"What you have to believe," Noella was saying, "is that I died instead of Noely."

Nanny pushed back her chair and got up from the table.

"All I can say is no good'll come from this play-actin'!"

Nanny spoke harshly, but Noella knew that she had agreed because there was nothing else she could do.

"Mr. Raven will be back as soon as he has had luncheon," she said to Nanny, "so I suggest we pack quickly what we have to take with us."

"We'll do nothin' of the sort 'til you've had something to eat!" Nanny said. "There's only soup, but there's a baby rabbit in it, so small as one can hardly see it, but at least it's better than nothin'!"

"Very well, Nanny, I will go into the Dining-Room," Noella said obediently.

She would have been quite willing to have her meals in the kitchen, but Nanny would never allow it.

"As long as I'm on my feet you'll behave like a lady," she had said when Noella had suggested it.

Now she went into the Dining-Room in which almost the only thing that was left was a side-table with two of its legs broken and only roughly repaired.

No-one had wanted to buy it and it now stood in the centre of the room.

Apart from that there were just two deal chairs to sit on, and it was here that Noella ate her meals because Nanny thought it was correct.

There was however a clean cloth on the table and a napkin beside a glass of water which Nanny had left ready for her.

She waited and a few minutes later Nanny came in with a soup-plate in which there was her luncheon and a small piece of stale bread to dip into it.

Nanny set it down on the table, and then as Noella picked up her spoon to eat the soup while it was still hot, she said;

"I've been talkin' it over with Mr. Hawkins, an' we thinks you'd do better without us. 'Raps we can manage somehow to stay here, where we at least has a roof over our heads."

Noella was aware that both Nanny and Hawkins were thinking that anything would be better than having to go to the Workhouse.

She looked up at Nanny and thought that no one could be more considerate or kinder than they were being.

"If you stay, I stay!" she declared. "I have already told Mr. Raven that I will not go to Yorkshire without you!"

Before Nanny could speak she went on:

"You, Nanny, are the only family I have left, my real family. You are part of me, wherever I may be, whatever I do, and you know I cannot lose you!"

She saw the tears come into Nanny's eyes.

But she said in her usual tart voice that had nevertheless a little tremor in it:

"If that's your attitude, then the sooner I starts packing, the better!"

She went out of the room and Noella quickly finished her soup and ran to join her.

There was really very little to pack, just the best of her gowns which were all threadbare and extremely shabby and two elaborate evening-gowns which had belonged to Noely.

She put on a dress with a cape over it which had belonged to her mother because it seemed more suitable than anything else she owned in which to travel.

Wearing her mother's best bonnet in which she had gone to Church, Noella felt more or less respectable.

Yet when she looked at herself in the mirror which was just a piece of glass without a frame, the dressing-table having been sold, she said to Nanny;

"I shall certainly look like the 'Beggar-Maid' arriving at the Palace of King Cophetua, but I do not suppose it will matter."

"Let's hope His Lordship'll kill the fatted calf for the Prodigal's return!" Nanny replied, and Noella could not help laughing.

When Mr. Raven returned he brought with him a pork-pie he had purchased at the Posting House.

He told them to eat it quickly because he was in a hurry to be off.

But while Noella could only manage a few mouthfuls Nanny and Hawkins ate every crumb that was left.

Before they had finished Mr. Raven was shouting that the horses were getting restless.

When Hawkins finally turned the key in the front door and handed it to Noella, she felt as if she must be dreaming.

Could she really be leaving the house in which she had been born and which had been her home for eighteen years?

Was she really going away with a strange man she had seen for the first time only a few hours ago?

Could she really be intending to impersonate Noely who lay beside her mother in the Churchyard.

"It is a crazy idea!" she told herself.

Yet at the same time she could not help a little surge of excitement. Everything had changed as if Mr. Raven had waved a magic-wand.

At least she need no longer go on worrying as to where her next meal was coming from.

Then as she looked at Nanny sitting on the small seat of the carriage opposite her, she told herself that however reprehensible it might be, she had done the right thing.

How could she leave two such kind people to starve?

She thought that just because he had eaten a little good food there had been a buoyancy in Hawkins as he swung himself up onto the box of the carriage.

There was also a touch of colour in Nanny's lined cheeks which had not been there this morning.

"I may be acting a lie, Mama," she said in her heart to her mother, "but at least I am doing something to help Nanny and Hawkins."

She had the strange feeling that her mother was smiling at her.

Only as they drove on did she think there was a kind of cynical complacency about Mr. Jasper Raven.

He was like a man who had won a battle single-handed, or rather had solved all his problems very much to his own satisfaction.

"Perhaps it will all come right in the end," she consoled herself.

Then she settled down to enjoy driving through the countryside in a luxurious manner that she had never known before.

Chapter Three

Jasper Raven took Noella to London.

They had to stay the night at a Posting House on the way, and she noted that he engaged the best rooms and a private Sitting-Room in which to eat their dinner.

The food was not particularly good, but it was certainly very much more plentiful than they had eaten for a long time.

After dinner she slept peacefully.

She knew that Nanny, although she did not say so, also had enjoyed a large dinner and a good night's rest.

When they set off the next morning, Noella realised that she was not as nervous as she had been the previous day.

They reached London late in the evening, having changed horses twice on the way, and as they drove into the City Jasper Raven said;

"I am taking you for the night to your brother's house in Park Street. He opened it for a short time last year, and when he left took all the staff with him except for two caretakers. There is no need therefore for you to be anxious about whom you might meet."

"I will . . try not to . . be," Noella said in a low voice.

"The caretakers will of course be told that you are Lady Noella," Jasper Raven said sharply, "and we shall have to have somewhat of a picnic dinner, but I bought some food and wine at the last place we stopped."

Noella thanked him for his forethought, and she also was aware that he was organising everything very skilfully, including herself.

She thought it was wrong, and at the same time, she knew she did not particularly like Jasper Raven.

At first she thought it was because she was shy of his smart appearance, and the fact that he obviously moved in a very different society from anything she had ever known.

Then she knew it was something deeper and more fundamental than that.

She could not really explain it to herself.

There was however something about him that made her feel that it had been a mistake to agree to his plan, even though it saved Nanny, Hawkins and herself from starvation.

When they arrived at the tall, rather imposing house in Park Street, she heard Jasper Raven giving sharp instructions to the caretakers who were obviously thrown into confusion at their unexpected arrival.

However, with Nanny and Hawkins to help, the beds were made up, and on Nanny's insistence hot bricks were rubbed over them in case they were damp.

By the time Noella had changed from her travelling-dress into the simple muslin gown she had worn at home, dinner, such as it was, was ready.

She had not thought of wearing one of Noely's gowns.

She thought they were far too elaborate and over-whelming for a quiet dinner with Jasper Raven.

In fact she thought he might laugh at her appearance and was therefore disconcerted when he said critically:

"Is that the best evening-gown you have?"

Noella blushed.

"It is the only one I have of my own," she replied, "but there are two of Noely's in my luggage which were too smart and elaborate to be saleable."

Jasper Raven looked her up and down in a manner which made her feel embarrassed. Then he said:

"I am wondering Noella, whether to buy you something decent in which to appear when we reach Raven Castle, or to leave you as you are."

46

"I think it would be more suitable to leave me as I am," Noella replied. "As you know, I have no money with which to buy anything, not even a handkerchief!"

She tried to speak lightly.

There was however, a note in her voice which would have told anyone who was not insensitive that she was fighting her tears.

She was not only tired, but once again she was feeling frightened of the deception in which she was involved.

She felt she was up against something large and menacing.

Actually it was the house that was more responsible for that than anything else.

It was dark and gloomy, and overpowering in a way she had not expected.

It seemed to her after living in the country that there was not a patch of colour anywhere, and she had a fore-boding that its owner would be like it.

Then she told herself she was being absurd.

It was not as if she had to face Noella's father, who had been a very autocratic man.

As the Earl was her 'brother' perhaps he would be glad to see her, and it would be exciting to talk to somebody near her own age.

They sat down in the large Dining-Room, the walls of which were panelled in dark oak.

On them were hanging portraits of Raven ancestors who, Noella felt, looked at her disapprovingly.

Hawkins waited on them and Noella had the idea that Nanny was helping in the kitchen.

She thought, because she was hungry, that the food was exceptionally good, although when dinner came to an end Jasper Raven said petulantly:

"If we had stayed in an Hotel, we would certainly have had more to eat!"

Noella did not reply.

She had had so little to eat for so long that the three courses were as much as she could manage.

Instead she said:

"Perhaps it would have been more expensive."

"That is immaterial!" Jasper Raven replied. "The Earl is going to reimburse me every penny I have expended on this trip, and a good deal more besides!"

The way he spoke made Noella feel uncomfortable.

Rising from the table she said:

"I am sure you will understand that, as I expect you wish to leave early in the morning, I would like to go to bed."

"That is a good idea," Jasper Raven agreed. "I shall go to my Club and find out what is the latest gossip."

Noella smiled.

"Do you think there will be any?"

"I should be very surprised if there is not!" Jasper Raven replied. "At the same time, now that King William is on the throne things are a great deal duller than when his brother was spending money like water!"

He laughed.

"The flambuoyant King George enjoyed having pretty women and a profusion of Bucks and Beaux round him!"

Noella clasped her hands together.

"Oh, please," she begged, "will you tell me about those days? It is something I have always longed to hear."

Jasper Raven smiled before he said;

"It is something you will certainly not hear spoken of in Yorkshire! However, I will try to tell you some tit-bits to cheer you up on our journey north."

It was only when she was undressed and in bed that Noella thought she was, if she was honest, afraid of what she would find at Raven Castle.

Supposing the Earl disliked her on sight? Or worse still, supposing he guessed when he saw her, that he was being deceived?

There was no reason why he should considering how alike she and Noely were.

At the same time, she knew she would have to be very

48

careful of what she said and watch every word in case she made a mistake.

She had a sudden impulse to jump out of bed and somehow find her way back to Worcestershire.

At least in the house she owned, however dilapidated it might be, she was not involved in lies or playing a part in which she might be exposed as a criminal.

She vaguely remembered at the back of her mind that Forgery was punishable by death.

Surely, if she pretended to be somebody other than herself, that was Forgery on a grand scale!

"I am afraid . . I am afraid, Mama!" she said in her heart to her mother.

Then with the tears still on her cheeks, because she was so tired, she fell asleep.

In the morning things seemed a little better.

The sunshine was coming through the high windows and there was a substantial breakfast in the Dining-Room.

Noella was sure that Nanny and Hawkins were enjoying the cups of tea of which they had been deprived.

When they were ready to leave she found that a different travelling-chariot was waiting outside.

It was twice the size of the one in which they had journeyed and was drawn by four horses.

Now there was plenty of room for Hawkins up on the box-seat.

Also Jasper Raven and herself could stretch out their legs without making it uncomfortable for Nanny, who was sitting opposite them.

Noella had the idea that Jasper Raven resented Nanny being with them, but there was nothing he could do about it.

Nanny however, was tactful enough to say little unless she was directly addressed.

The horses soon carried them out of London.

Once they were in open country on the road leading North, Noella found that there was much she wanted to see.

She therefore looked out of the window instead of questioning Jasper Raven as she had intended to do.

They reached Baldock in time for luncheon.

Then they were off again with a new team of horses that were as good as the ones with which they had started.

Even with four horses it took them three days to reach Yorkshire.

By the time they saw the bare, undulating hills, the lush valleys and the broad rivers, Noella was very tired.

Because she had been deprived of an adequate diet for so long, she had not the strength and resilience she should have had at her age.

She was also worried about Nanny, who looked exhausted although she had slept for a great deal of the journey.

Because it was impossible for her to sleep on the small seat of the carriage, Noella had insisted on their changing places.

"Now lie back in the corner, Nanny," she said, "and you can go to sleep. When you feel refreshed, I will do the same."

She had expected that Jasper Raven would argue over such an arrangement. However although she was aware that he felt resentful, he said nothing.

Whenever they stopped to change horses, there was a good meal available for them.

She noticed that Jasper Raven ordered the best claret for himself and followed it with several glasses of brandy.

She had learned that the footman on the box was his personal valet.

Although he was a cheeky little man whom she did not like, she had to give him credit for Jasper Raven's elegant appearance.

She had noticed that every morning his Hessian boots were shining like mirrors.

"We have only a few more miles to go now," Jasper Raven said unexpectedly.

Noella, who was admiring the view and thinking that Yorkshire was very beautiful, started.

She turned her large blue eyes towards him with a questioning look, and he said:

"Now try not to be nervous. Remember that the Earl, even if he seems frightening, is only your brother. And as he wants to see you, he must be looking forward eagerly to your arrival."

Noella hoped this was true.

At the same time she felt so apprehensive that it was like a heavy stone in her breast.

At just about three o'clock in the afternoon they turned in through two large and impressive wrought-iron gates with heraldic stone animals set on either side of them.

Noella felt breathless.

Now was the testing time, now was the moment when either her supposed brother would accept her, or she would be sent away in disgrace.

She knew that Nanny was feeling worried too.

She pulled at the black cape she wore over her grey gown, and made sure the ribbons that tied her bonnet under her chin were in place.

"Now you be very careful!" Jasper Raven said to Nanny in what Noella thought was a harsh voice. "One whisper from you or Hawkins that Lady Noella is not what she appears to be, and you will both be out in the street with nowhere to go except the Workhouse!"

The way he spoke seemed to Noella unnecessarily cruel.

She saw a sudden stricken look in Nanny's eyes, and knew it was with considerable effort that she did not make an angry retort.

Instead she said quietly:

"You know, Sir, that neither Hawkins nor me'd do anythin' to harm a hair of – Her Ladyship's head."

She stumbled a little over the word 'Ladyship'.

Because it was so unlike Nanny to speak in such a subservient way, Noella wanted to put her arms around her and kiss her.

But she knew that would undoubtedly bring a rebuke from Jasper Raven, so she merely reached out and laid her hand over Nanny's.

"This is an adventure, Nanny dear, so let us try to enjoy it."

"That is a sensible attitude," Jasper Raven approved, "but unless one takes care, an adventure can end in disaster!"

He was deliberately trying to frighten her, Noella thought, and she wanted to reply that, if the worst came to the worst, they could always go home.

Then she thought she was being ungrateful and merely said:

"You know I want to thank you, Cousin Jasper."

This was what he had told her to call him, because he was Noely's cousin and it was another thing she must remember when they reached the Castle.

Now after they had driven some way down the drive, the Castle was just ahead of them.

Her first impression was of a magnificent grey stone building with turrets and towers which made it look exactly like a Castle out of a Story-Book.

At the same time it was very large and impressive and she had the frightened feeling that its owner would be the same.

The horses came to a standstill in front of a flight of wide steps.

They led up to the porticoed front door which was opened immediately on their arrival.

A red carpet was run down the steps by two liveried footmen as another footman opened the carriage door.

He was wearing a white wig which was something Noella had never seen before, and as she and Jasper walked slowly up the steps to the front door, there was a grey-haired Butler waiting for them.

He bowed respectfully to Jasper saying:

"Good-afternoon, Sir, and you, M'Lady. His Lordship anticipated you would arrive some time this afternoon."

"Is His Lordship waiting for us?" Jasper enquired.

"His Lordship is in the Library, Sir," the Butler replied.

He walked ahead of them and Noella was able to take in at a quick glance the huge marble mantelpiece in the Hall.

Over it hung tattered flags which she guessed had been won in battle by Ravens who had taken part in them.

There was a wide corridor hung with pictures and containing some extremely fine English furniture which she recognised from books she had read in the Vicar's library.

Her Governess had also described the fine furniture in the ancestral home in which she had taught her previous pupils.

It was difficult however to think of anything except the man who owned this Castle, who had paid for her to come to Yorkshire believing her to be his sister, and was now waiting to see her.

She heard the Butler announce in stentorian tones:

"Mr. Jasper Raven, M'Lord!"

Noella guessed that she was not announced because the Butler was not certain if it was correct for him to do so.

This, she knew, was the testing point; the moment when she stayed or was sent away in disgrace.

She found herself unable to look at the tall man who rose from the desk near the window.

He seemed unnaturally large as he walked towards them, and because Noella was shy she dared not look up into his face.

Then she heard him say in a deep voice:

"So you have arrived, Jasper! I hope it was not too arduous a journey?"

"It was very tiring," Jasper replied, "but at the same time very satisfactory!"

He paused as if to make what he said more dramatic.

"May I present you to your sister Noella?"

He stood to one side and indicated her.

As she raised her eyes to the Earl's she had a sudden feeling that she was standing alone on the very edge of a deep gulf.

She did not know what she expected him to look like, but she thought perhaps he would have some resemblance to Noely and his mother.

In fact, on the contrary it would have been impossible to guess there was any relationship between them.

It flashed through her mind that of course he was exactly like his father, and there was no doubt he was definitely frightening.

His hair was dark and he was, she supposed, extremely handsome.

His steel-grey eyes looked at her, she thought, scrutinisingly as he held out his hand, and he was not smiling.

"Welcome to the Castle, Noella," he said, "which of course you cannot remember."

Noella put her hand into his, but his fingers did not close over hers.

"I expect," the Earl went on, "that after such a long journey you would like to change. I suggest you are shown up to your bedroom while Cousin Jasper tells me in what circumstances he found you."

"Thank you," Noella murmured.

The Earl looked to where the Butler was still standing in the doorway.

"Take Her Ladyship to Mrs. Kirkton."

"Very good, M'Lord."

Noella felt herself dismissed.

It was somewhat of an anti-climax after what she had anticipated her meeting with the Earl would be like.

She went back along the wide corridor and the Butler led the way up the stairs at the top of which was waiting the Housekeeper.

She was an elderly woman with grey hair, who dropped her a curtsy.

"You must be tired, M'Lady," the Housekeeper said as they walked along another wide corridor. "Everyone as

54

comes here from the South says what an exhausting journey it is, but well worth the effort once they gets here."

"I am sure that is true," Noella said.

Mrs. Kirkton opened the door to a large, very attractive room.

There was a huge four-poster bed draped with exquisitely embroidered curtains.

There were two long windows which looked out over what Noella realised was a formal garden.

There was a fountain throwing its water iridescent, high into the air, and as it caught the sunshine, it looked so beautiful that she drew in her breath.

Mrs. Kirkton followed the direction of her eyes.

"Everyone admires our garden," she said, "and t'was his late Lordship's pride and joy. I know Your Ladyship'll want to see the Maze and the Grotto which is lined entirely with sea-shells."

"It all sounds very exciting!" Noella exclaimed.

Mrs. Kirkton went on talking as she helped Noella out of her travelling clothes.

Her dress and cape in such luxurious surroundings looked even more shabby than they had when she left Worcestershire.

Her luggage had been brought upstairs and was being unpacked by two maid-servants in starched white aprons and caps.

Her clothes were hung in the large wardrobe which was surmounted by a golden bird which she knew was the Raven crest.

It was then that Mrs. Kirkton said tentatively:

"Is this all you have with you, M'Lady?"

"It is all I possess," Noella replied.

Mrs. Kirkton lifted down one of her gowns which had faded during all the years she had worn it, and was also darned in several places.

She did not say anything, but Noella realised how horrified she was that any Raven should be so poverty-stricken.

There was however nothing she could do about it, and when Noella had put on the gown, then Mrs. Kirkton arranged her hair.

She was already aware that the way she wore it was unfashionable, as she was feeling embarrassed, she did not realised that the pale gold made her look unusual and at the same time very lovely.

With her huge eyes filling her face, it would have been impossible for anyone who looked at her not to want to look again and go on looking.

She was only conscious that her trunk was empty and her few and worn out gowns were hanging in the wardrobe.

They seemed almost ludicrous beside the carved gold posts of the bed with its beautiful curtains.

"Thank you very much for helping me," Noella said to the Housekeeper and smiled at the two maids who had unpacked for her.

She walked to the bedroom door, then hesitated.

"Shall I join His Lordship in the Library?" she asked.

"Mr. Johnson'll be waiting for you in the hall, M'Lady, and I thinks you'll find His Lordship is in the Drawing-Room where tea'll be served."

That was good news, as Noella felt it was a long time since she had eaten luncheon, which had not been a particularly good one.

Then she almost laughed at herself for being critical.

A week ago she would have gobbled up gladly anything she was offered and certainly would not have been particular. Now as Nanny would say, she could 'pick and choose'.

At least she would not go hungry in the Castle, nor would Nanny and Hawkins and that, she told herself, was more important than anything else.

"I have to be grateful that we are here, there are no bills to pay, and we are no longer starving," she told herself.

She reached the bottom of the stairs and Johnson the Butler said;

"His Lordship's in the Drawing-Room, M'Lady, and he thought after your journey you'd be glad of a cup of tea."

"It sounds very nice," Noella replied, "and I hope that Nanny is all right."

"Miss Browning has been looked after," the Butler assured her, "and so has the man-servant Your Ladyship brought with you."

"Hawkins was . . .!"

Noella was just about to say: "Hawkins was Batman to my father," when she remembered and bit back the words.

For a moment she felt panic-stricken.

How could she have been so stupid as to be on the very edge of making a gaffe such a short time after she had arrived?

She was so frightened at having nearly betrayed herself that when the Butler showed her into the Drawing-Room she could only stand for a moment just inside the door wondering what she should do.

Then she realised that at the end of the room the Earl and Jasper Raven were sitting in comfortable armchairs at the fireside.

Near them was a table laid for tea with all the silver that Noella could remember her mother having when she was a child.

On a large silver tray there was a kettle with a lighted wick burning beneath it and a silver teapot, cream jug and sugar basin to match.

There was also, and they used one like it for many years before it finally had to be sold, a little Queen Anne silver container.

This was what the tea had originally been locked away in because it was so precious.

It was only opened by the hostess with a special key.

"I am waiting for you to pour out the tea, Noella," the Earl said, and again she thought it was more of a command than a request.

She sat down at the tea-table and obediently filled the beautiful Crown Derby cups.

At the same time Noella was aware that on the table and on the 'Dumb-Waiter' which consisted of five little shelves, there was a feast!

Hot scones were in a covered silver dish, sandwiches of several kinds filled three plates, and a variety of cakes which filled several others.

There were fairy-cakes such as her mother used to make when she was a child, and there was also a heavy fruit cake, a sponge decorated with cherries, a chocolate cake, and a cake with pink and white icing.

Because the Earl was talking to Jasper neither of them paid much attention to her.

Noella was able to eat in which she confessed to herself was a greedy manner and enjoyed every mouthful.

"One thing is quite certain," she told herself with a little smile, "I shall grow very fat at the Castle if I stay here very long."

"And what Noella, do you think of your home now that you have seen it?" the Earl asked unexpectedly.

Noella started.

"It is . . bigger than I . . expected," she replied, "and I think . . the fountain in the garden is very . . beautiful."

"You do not remember it?"

The question was sharp.

"No . . I am afraid not," Noella replied truthfully.

The Earl rose.

"Come and look at the rose-garden," he said. "Our grandfather was very proud of the roses he grew."

Noella walked across the room to join him at the window.

She was aware as she did so that Jasper Raven was watching them.

She thought it was embarrassing to know that he was listening attentively to everything she said, ready to criticise and perhaps, when he got the opportunity, rebuke her.

'I wish he would go away,' she thought to herself, 'it would be much easier here without him.'

She turned her back on him to look at the rose-garden through the open window.

The roses were not yet in bloom but she could see how skilfully the bushes had been arranged around an ancient sun-dial.

There were little flagged paths bordering the rose-beds and beyond them was a long stretch of green lawn stretching down to a yew-hedge.

It was surmounted by birds trimmed in topiary which Noella supposed represented ravens.

It was so lovely, so different from what she had expected, and she could only stare at what she saw.

Then she was aware that the Earl was looking at her.

"I suppose," he said after a moment, "that you were expecting like most people, to find Yorkshire wild, primitive, and perhaps uncivilised."

"No .. of course .. not," Noella replied. "At the same time, I did not expect it to be quite so .. beautiful!"

There was silence.

Then the Earl said with what she thought was a mocking note in his voice:

"Are you comparing what you see here with the gardens of the Palaces and Villas in Italy, which must be even more impressive, or perhaps the bougainvillaea in Monte Carlo."

For a moment Noella did not understand what he was saying.

Then she remembered that those were the places where he knew Noely had lived.

With an effort she managed to reply:

"Perhaps because I am English, I am finding English gardens and English scenery more beautiful than anywhere else in the .. world."

She could not help as she spoke looking towards Jasper.

She saw a faint twist to his lips and a look of approval in his eyes, and knew she had been clever.

59

Almost as if the Earl was disappointed that she did not have a different point of view, he turned away from the window saying:

"I think it would be a mistake to show you any more now. Tomorrow there will be plenty of time for you to explore the Castle and some of the gardens."

"I am longing to see it all," Noella said.

The Earl looked at the clock on the mantelpiece.

"And now, I suppose," he said, "you should rest before dinner, which will be at seven-thirty. If you feel too tired to join us, tell your maid to let me know and dinner will be sent to you upstairs."

"I would like to join you," Noella said firmly.

She thought it would be a mistake to do anything unusual on her first night.

At the same time, she was glad of the opportunity to lie down.

"If I get over-tired," she told herself, "I shall be more likely to make mistakes, as I nearly did just now. I must be careful."

She said the same words over and over to herself as the maid helped her undress and she got into bed.

Even as she shut her eyes she was saying:

"I must be careful."

She repeated it until she fell asleep.

Downstairs Jasper Raven said to the Earl:

"I had better return this miniature to you. As you see, Noely is still very like it."

"Her fair gold hair is certainly unusual," the Earl said dryly.

Jasper Raven put the miniature down on a small table beside him. Then he said:

"And now, Lyndon, what about the telescope? You did promise to finance it if I found your sister."

There was a pause before the Earl replied:

"In your absence I took your plans to an expert in London."

Jasper frowned.

"You did not tell me you were going to do that."

"I should have thought you might have anticipated I would be businesslike about something which involves a considerable sum of money!" the Earl remarked.

"The plans were of course only in the preliminary stage before further development," Jasper said.

"*Very* preliminary, I imagine," the Earl replied. "The expert I consulted told me they were far from being new or original."

Jasper stiffened and sat upright.

"I do not believe it!"

"That is what I was told," the Earl answered, "and to confirm it I consulted the head of the Research Committee of both the Army and the Navy."

"In which case they are doubtless jealous that anyone should discover anything before they have!"

"I do not think it is a question of jealousy!" the Earl replied. "They simply already have a telescope which is superior in every way to the one you have suggested producing."

Jasper got to his feet to stand looking down into the fire with his back to the Earl.

After a moment the latter said:

"I am sorry about this, Jasper. It was a good try on your part, but I am not as stupid as most of your victims."

Jasper turned round.

"Damn you!" he said. "I might have known you would be as close-fisted as your father."

"It is not a question of being close-fisted," the Earl said, "but of being businesslike, and I dislike throwing money down a drain."

"Which I suppose you are insinuating I am!"

"At the moment I am not being personal," the Earl said in a lofty tone. "I am merely telling you that I will not invest my money in anything that has not a chance of showing a return and which is laughed at by those qualified to assess its worth!"

For a moment Jasper glared at him.

With an effort he restrained himself from speaking the words which came to his lips and instead said sullenly:

"Then what do I get for having found your sister for you?"

"I thought it would be fair," the Earl replied, "to pay of course your expenses, though they seem to me somewhat extortionate, and to give you two thousand pounds for your services."

"£2,000, when I asked for £10,000?" Jasper expostulated.

The Earl did not reply, but merely looked at his cousin contemptuously.

"I suppose I have no alternative but to accept it!" Jasper said after a long silence.

"That is entirely up to you."

"Why can you not do the gracious thing and give me £5,000?"

"Because quite frankly, Jasper," the Earl answered, "I do not want a scandal in the family, you have had a lot of money out of me already."

Jasper made an impatient sound, but he did not speak, and the Earl went on:

"Enough is enough, and actually I resent being treated as such an ignoramus that I would fall for so obvious a confidence trick on your part!"

"All right, that was a mistake," Jasper agreed. "But if you are afraid of a scandal, then unless you pay up my debts, you are going to have one. I owe at least twice what you have offered me!"

"You are not the only member of the family who needs money," the Earl pointed out. "And there are, as you are well aware, a great many other commitments that I cannot ignore."

"I know, I know!" Jasper said irritably. "The Alms-Houses, the Schools, the old-age pensioners! I have heard it all before!"

"You are perfectly welcome to read the Account-Books

and see what it all costs," the Earl said patiently. "Then you will understand that one Raven can overspend to the detriment of the whole family."

"It is easy for you to talk like that," Jasper said. "You have been brought up in luxury! You have never known what it is to be without food, and be down to your last penny! To have people hammering on your door to be paid!"

The Earl did not speak, and Jasper continued:

"You might ask your sister what it is like to be hungry, as she was when I arrived at the house that looked as if it was going to collapse about her ears at any moment!"

His voice rose as he said:

"She had virtually nothing to eat or drink and, as you can see, even after the last few days when I have fed her like a prize sow, she is still only skin and bone!"

"You can hardly apply that description to yourself!" the Earl said.

"My position is just as bad!" Jasper snapped. "I only hope you will feel proud when I am taken to a Debtors' prison!"

"This is what you said to me the last time I paid your bills." the Earl retorted. "You must realise, Jasper, that you cannot go on like this!"

"My God! What I am asking is little enough!" Jasper said. "I am a Raven as you are, and as a Raven I am entitled to some of the vast wealth which you are able to use to your own advantage."

He spat the words, and the Earl rose to his feet.

"I am not going to argue with you, Jasper," he said, "and because you have brought my sister home, I will for the last time help you by making out a cheque for £5,000. When that is all gone, please do not come back asking for more, because as far as I am concerned, you have had the last penny you will ever extract from me! Do you understand?"

"You make it perfectly clear," Jasper said, "and I would like the money immediately, in case you change your mind, before I leave tomorrow morning."

The Earl's lips twisted in a wry smile before he replied:

"If you do not trust me, I assure you I have not trusted you for years, and with good reason! I can only hope that after tomorrow we do not meet again."

As he spoke he walked from the Drawing-Room leaving Jasper alone.

For a moment Jasper stood with his back to the fire-place staring at the closed door through which the Earl had left.

Then he walked across to the window to stare out at the sun setting behind the trees, and the sun-dial throwing a long shadow over the rose-garden.

"Damn him! Damn him!" he swore beneath his breath. "May he rot in hell! One day, I will make him pay for this!"

Chapter Four

Noella opened her eyes and found that she had been awoken by Nanny drawing back the curtains.

For a moment she could not remember where she was.

Then with a start she realised that she had been asleep for a very long time, and had missed dinner with the Earl.

She sat up in bed saying as she did so:

"How could you let me sleep for so long?"

"I came to call you before dinner," Nanny answered, arranging the curtains neatly as she spoke, "and you were tired out, so I refused to wake you."

"Oh, Nanny, I am sure that was a mistake!" Noella said. "Perhaps I should have made an effort to go down."

"Why should you ?" Nanny asked. "After a journey which almost killed us – it was so tiring!"

Nanny spoke with so much feeling that Noella realised it had been too much for her.

She was aware that the reason really was that they had been weakened through having so little food.

When Nanny fetched her breakfast-tray on which there was a dish of eggs and bacon, as well as toast, honey and a choice of several fruits, she could only smile.

How could she have imagined a week ago when she was wondering how they could afford even a little stale bread that she would now be having food like this?

Only when she had finished everything that was on the tray did she ask the time.

"It is half after ten!" Nanny replied.

Noella gave a little cry.

"Surely the Earl will think it very rude of me to be so late?"

"His Lordship's gone riding, if that's what's worrying you!" Nanny said, a dry note in her voice.

Then as Noella did not answer, she said in a voice little above a whisper:

"This is a strange house for all its comfort and good food!"

"What do you mean by that?" Noella asked.

"I don't know exactly," Nanny answered, "but the Housekeeper was tellin' me that His Lordship never got over losing his mother."

Noella looked at Nanny wide-eyed.

"You mean he resented her running away?"

"It almost broke 'is heart at the time, they say, and his father, the late Earl, brought him up to mistrust all women."

Noella was listening carefully to everything Nanny had to tell her and after a moment she said:

"If he feels like that, why was he anxious to have his sister here?"

"As far as I can make out," Nanny replied, "they've all bin puzzling about that, seeing as how his relatives have been begging him to get married and produce an heir."

"But he has refused because he dislikes women?" Noella enquired.

"They're not saying as how he dislikes them," Nanny replied, "it's just that he don't trust them, and who can blame him for that?"

She looked at Noella, thinking how lovely she looked with the sunshine coming in through the high window, and said:

"Oh, Dearie, I wish you weren't here pretending to be someone you ain't. It's wrong, that's what it is!"

"I know, Nanny," Noella replied, "and we have talked about it before. But there was nothing we could do, except get hungrier and hungrier."

66

She gave a deep sigh before she said:

"I cannot believe Mama or Papa would want that to happen."

Nanny pressed her lips together as if she wanted to say a great deal more but thought better of it.

Then she changed the subject, saying:

"I'll tell them you're ready for your bath; then you must go downstairs and wait for His Lordship."

Noella felt as if a little shaft of fear ran through her at what she had to do.

Then she was intrigued as the housemaids came in first to light the fire in the grate, then they spread a large bath-mat in front of it and placed on it a circular bath.

While they were doing this, footmen were bringing up large brass cans filled with hot water which they left just outside the door.

The housemaids poured the hot water into a bath and added a few drops of perfume which they said was distilled from violets.

Noella got out of bed.

She felt as she soaked in the scented water that she had never enjoyed a bath more.

Nanny wrapped her in a large white bath-towel and helped her to dry.

She wanted to laugh because it was so different from anything she had experienced before.

It was an anticlimax when she put on one of the faded and threadbare gowns she had worn for years.

"You'd better persuade His Lordship to let you have some new clothes!" Nanny remarked. "Otherwise you'll soon be walking about naked!"

It was something Nanny had said before, and then there had been no answer to the question: where was the money to pay for them?

Now Noella could not help thinking she would be far better dressed if she wore one of the curtains from the window, or even a table-cloth.

She however, kissed Nanny and said:

"This is an adventure, and we can only wait to see what happens."

Nanny was going to make one of her tart retorts when a maid came into the room.

"His Lordship is back from riding and wishes to see Her Ladyship," she said.

"I am ready," Noella said. "I will go downstairs at once!"

She hurried out of the room and down the wide corridor, only stopping at the top of the magnificent carved staircase to look down into the hall.

On the walls as well as pictures there was a set of tapestries representing the four seasons.

Below them stood some antique statuary which she knew would be exciting to look at when she had the time.

She was sure that each one had a history.

There was more statuary in the corridor which led to the Library where she was told the Earl was waiting for her.

She had been too bemused last night to notice them, but now she saw Ceres the Roman Goddess of plenty, and thought her presence was certainly appropriate at Raven Castle.

Johnson opened the door of the Library, and as if to make up for his omission of yesterday he announced:

"Lady Noella, M'Lord!"

Noella was able to take a quick glance at the huge collection of books which made the walls a kaleidoscope of colour.

Then she had eyes only for the Earl who was standing looking out of the window.

He was still wearing his riding-clothes and she thought no man could look more handsome, or smarter.

He was wearing white breeches, a cut-away coat, and riding-boots which had been polished until they reflected the furniture.

"Good morning, Noella!" he said, as she walked towards him. "I hope you slept well."

"I can only apologise," Noella replied, "for sleeping for so long, and missing dinner last night."

"You must have been very tired," the Earl said. "Actually, you missed nothing except our Cousin Jasper sulking."

Noella for a moment looked surprised, then she asked:

"Did you refuse to finance his telescope?"

"So he told you about that!"

"Yes, he seemed very anxious that you should help him."

There was a twist to the Earl's lips as he retorted:

"I am sure he was! But I am used to his tricks to extract money from me, and this is the last time!"

There was a hard note in his voice which Noella did not miss and she was silent until the Earl said:

"Come and sit down. I want to talk to you."

Noella moved towards the fireplace and seated herself deliberately in a high-backed armchair rather than on a more comfortable sofa.

She had the feeling that what she was about to hear would not be particularly pleasant.

Why she should think so, she had no idea.

The Earl moved to stand with his back to the fire.

She was aware that his grey eyes were looking at her penetratingly as if he searched beneath the surface.

It made her nervous and then, even though she was sure it was impossible for him to read her thoughts, she was afraid.

She looked up at him apprehensively, and clenched her hands in her lap.

"First of all," the Earl said, "I should explain why the letter to your father was not answered sooner."

"The one I wrote from Venice," Noella murmured, remembering what Noely had told her.

"When it arrived he was very ill, very ill indeed," the Earl said, "and I was abroad, so it was therefore set on one side."

"I . . I thought something . . like that . . might have been the . . explanation," Noella said.

She remembered how bitter Noela had been that her

69

father had ignored her, and she wished she could tell her it had not been deliberate.

"When after his death I was finally able to attend to his correspondence," the Earl said. "I wrote to you in Venice, and thought as there was no reply, you must have left."

"We had gone to Naples," Noella said in a low voice.

"That is what Jasper told me. He said he had difficulty in tracing you, and from there, I understand, you came to England to stay with your mother's old friends."

"Mama and .. Mrs. Wakefield were cousins, and had grown up together," Noella said.

She thought as she spoke that she was being clever in speaking confidently of what had occurred so that the Earl would not be suspicious.

"And when you were there, I understand," the Earl continued, "your mother died."

He had said 'your mother' instead of speaking of her as his.

Noella knew there was a hard note in his voice which could be accounted for by what Nanny had just told her.

She thought it best to say nothing.

She only looked down at her hands, her eye-lashes long on her cheeks, hiding her eyes.

"I understand that you do not wish to talk about it," the Earl went on, "and neither do I. In fact, I do not intend to mention your mother again, or hear anything about her."

There was no doubt now, Noella thought, that he did indeed hate his mother, and the way he spoke was harsh and aggressive.

Because she was trying to think how Noely would have reacted to his attitude she said quietly:

"She was .. your mother too .. and after Captain Fairburn died .. she suffered .. terribly."

"I do not wish to hear about it!" the Earl retorted sharply. "If she suffered it was only what she deserved. She behaved abominably! How could any woman worthy

70

of the name leave her husband for a gambling scallywag –
and her son!"

There was a pause before the last three words and
Noella knew that was the whole explanation for his
attitude.

His mother had taken her daughter with her, but left
her only son behind.

Surely, she thought, she must have loved him?

Surely it must have been a terrible wrench to creep
away when she knew how much he would miss her.

"But all that is in the past," the Earl was saying in a
different tone. "What you have to do now, Noella, is to
make certain that you are free of your mother's bad
influence and become worthy of being your father's
daughter."

As he finished speaking, he walked from the fireplace
across the room to his desk and back again.

"I have been thinking this over very carefully," he went
on, "and I wish to make it clear from the very beginning
that I will not countenance any behaviour on your part
which reflects the life you have been living."

He drew in his breath and went on:

"It was deplorable, in fact, to my mind absolutely
abominable, that a young girl should have been involved
in a sin committed by her mother, and a life based on the
gambling hells of Europe!"

Noella listened wide-eyed.

She had known that people were shocked by the
licentiousness of the Venetians, who thought only of
pleasure.

She also vaguely, because Noely had said so, knew that
the extravagance of the rich in Rome was in stark contrast
to the life of the very poor in Naples and many other
Italian Cities.

But she knew little about them and wondered how they
could in any way, have contaminated Noely.

Thinking therefore she must somehow stand up for
Noely and her mother, she said:

"I think you are being needlessly apprehensive about such places and I actually never went into any Casinos nor did I have anything to do with gamblers."

"How can you say that," the Earl demanded, "when you were living in the same house as D'Arcy Fairburn? Do not pretend to me, Noella! He was a compulsive gambler, a seducer of women, and a swine to whom no decent man should speak!"

There was deep condemnation in the Earl's words.

What he said sounded even worse because although he spoke vehemently his voice was not loud, but sharp and as cutting as a whip.

For a moment the very air seemed to vibrate with his fury.

Then Noella said hesitantly:

"Perhaps . . as you feel like that . . it was a . . mistake for me to . . come here . . and I . . I should go . . away."

As she spoke she wondered frantically what, if he agreed, she could do, or where she could go.

"You will stay here," the Earl said firmly, "and I will make sure that you no longer remain in the gutter in which you have been living, or consort with anyone except people of whom I approve."

He was standing once more in front of the fire as he continued:

"I intend to instruct you on how you should behave and how you should think and then, when I consider you are no longer tainted by those with whom you have been associating, I will find you a husband!"

"A . . A husband?" Noella faltered.

"Naturally it will be someone of whom I approve, but it may not be as easy as it should be owing to the life you have led since you left here as a child."

"Please," Noella said in a voice that trembled, "I have no wish . . to . . marry anyone until I . . fall in love."

"Love?" the Earl ejaculated. "What do you know of love? Except that a deceitful and degraded woman carried you away from your home and allowed you to be brought

72

up in the most regrettable surroundings and left in abject poverty!"

The words seemed to come from his lips like shots from a pistol.

Then he turned towards her and said:

"Look at yourself! Look what love has done for you!"

Noella gave a little gasp and he continued:

"You are wearing a gown that would be discarded by a kitchen-maid. You are far too thin from lack of food and you possess nothing except rags!"

He paused to say forceably:

"Let me reiterate once and for all that love is a disaster, and it is something of which you should be ashamed!"

The attack was so surprising that Noella could only stare at him, her eyes seeming to fill her whole face.

Yet at the back of her mind she could understand why he was speaking like this.

Why for him the love his mother had for D'Arcy Fairburn was unclean.

Feeling there was nothing she could say, she sat still.

Her hands were clenched together until the knuckles showed white, her face was very pale, and there was an expression of fear in her eyes.

As if he was suddenly aware that he was striking at something small and vulnerable, the Earl gave an exasperated exclamation and walked to the window.

He stood looking out with what Noella was sure were unseeing eyes.

After a long, embarrassing silence, she said in a very small voice:

"I . . I am . . sorry."

"For yourself?" the Earl asked without turning round.

"No . . for you . . you have suffered . . and I can . . understand it has made you very . . bitter."

She thought he was surprised, but he did not say so.

Then after another long silence when she wondered if it would be best for her to go away, he turned round.

"The first thing we have to do," he said in a rather

73

different tone of voice, "is to provide you with a whole new wardrobe of clothes."

Because she felt he was making an effort, Noella managed to reply:

"That .. would be very .. exciting! I was thinking when I was dressing that I would look .. better if I was wearing .. one of the .. curtains in this wonderful Castle, or perhaps .. if you could spare it .. a tapestry!"

The Earl laughed, and she felt it was a reluctant sound, but as if he could not help himself.

"I think that would make you look rather strange," he said. "Actually I have already sent a carriage to York to bring back the best Dressmaker in the City."

Noella gave a little murmur, as he went on:

"Perhaps later we will go to London, but for the moment it would be a mistake for anybody to see you until you are dressed as befits your position as my sister."

"That will be .. wonderful for me," Noella said, "and please .. may I ask you .. something?"

"Of course!"

"Could you .. give Nanny and Hawkins some .. money? They have not been paid any .. wages for a long .. time."

She thought there was a frown between the Earl's eyes and she added:

"Please .. be generous."

The Earl thought for a moment, then he said:

"I presume the woman you call 'Nanny' was a servant of Mrs. Wakefield, and Hawkins her man-servant."

Noella realised this was something she should have thought of before or rather Cousin Jasper should have thought of, for her.

She searched frantically for an explanation and after a moment she said:

"You are quite right. Nanny was with Mrs. Wakefield, but she was absolutely .. marvellous in looking after .. Mama until she .. died."

74

The Earl was scowling at the mention of his mother and she went on quickly:

"Hawkins kept us alive by bringing in the wood for the fire, and snaring rabbits which were . . all we . . had to . . eat."

Her voice trembled as she said:

"I know that . . without them . . I would have . . died too."

The frown vanished from between the Earl's eyes.

"In which case," he said, "of course they must be rewarded, and I can understand now why you could not leave them behind."

"If I had done so," Noella replied, "the only place they would have been able to go to . . was the . . Workhouse!"

"Forget it!" the Earl said. "Forget what you have been through and of course those who have looked after you may continue to do so."

"Thank you, thank you!" Noella cried. "It is what I want more than . . anything else!"

"More than some new gowns?"

"I hope I may have those too, and as you have already pointed out, looking as I am, even your statues are affronted by my appearance!"

She thought there was a faint smile on the Earl's lips and went on:

"I am quite . . sure that Ceres gave me a most . . disdainful look as I passed her . . just now!"

The Earl laughed as if he could not help himself and said:

"I am surprised that you should recognise her. Now, come and be introduced to some of the other notabilities in the Castle."

"That will be very . . thrilling!" Noella said. "And I hope you will allow me to read all the books you have in this room."

"All of them?" the Earl questioned.

"If you give me your permission to do so, it will ensure that I am . . here for at least another . . hundred years!"

The Earl gave another of his sharp laughs, and she had the feeling it sounded a little strange because he was not often amused.

They walked round the Library and Noella found to her surprise that while there were books that were very ancient, there were also "Women as they are," by Mrs. Gore, Edward Bulwer Lytton's fifth novel and the poems of Lord Byron.

She did not however let the Earl know that she recognised the last, feeling he would disapprove of her reading anything that was about love.

She therefore let him lead her from the Library into the long Gallery.

It was filled with magnificent portraits by Van Dyck, Sir Peter Lely, and Gainsborough.

As they were what she had always wanted to see, she ran from one picture to another excitedly.

She was enthralled by a very fine portrait of Queen Henrietta Maria by Van Dyck.

She was intrigued by one of the Duke of Albemarle who was both an Admiral and a General, which had been painted by Sir Godfrey Kneller.

She did not realise that the Earl was surprised to find how much she knew about the artists.

Later he was astounded when they inspected the silver cabinet and she talked of Sir Martin Bowes and Adam and Paul Vianen of Elrecht who were the Master Silversmiths of the 16th century.

He was not to know that Mrs. Wakefield had loved pictures and had as a girl studied in depth the great artists of the past.

She had made Noella as knowledgeable as she was, not only about all forms of Art such as painting but also furniture, silver and music.

When they entered the Music Room, Noella gave a cry of delight at the sight of the piano.

"Oh, please," she begged, "will you allow me to play it sometimes?"

"Of course," the Earl answered, "but I did not expect you to be a musician!"

"That is rather a grand word for it," Noella laughed, "but I love playing, and when we did not have a piano, I used to play the organ in Church,"

"Then you are obviously an expert," the Earl said dryly. "But I hope your repertoire does not consist only of hymns!"

Noella wanted to reply that she could play not only the Sonatas of Chopin, but also the dreamy music of the Waltz.

The dance had been introduced to London by the Princess de Lieven during the reign of King George IV.

Then she thought before she spoke that perhaps the Earl would dislike that as something she had learnt in the places he condemned, such as Rome and Venice and above all in Paris.

She therefore said nothing.

She was on safer ground when they went into luncheon and she could admire the marvellous Dining-Room which had been decorated by Adam.

Standing against the pale green walls there were a pair of carved and gilt side tables which had been acquired in the reign of Charles II.

The pictures were so magnificent that she found it hard not to look at them rather than her food.

At the same time, everything she ate was delicious.

It was infuriating to find that because she had had so little to eat for so long, she had to refuse several dishes.

"I should have thought you would be hungry!" the Earl remarked as she finally refused the fruit that was offered her in an exquisite Sèvres porcelain dish.

"The truth is," Noella replied, "that I want to say yes, but in Nanny's words 'my eyes are bigger than my stomach', and I just cannot manage any more."

She spoke in the same way she would have spoken to her mother and thought the Earl looked rather surprised.

"Perhaps I should try to be more serious and ladylike," she told herself.

Then because it was impossible for her to be anything but natural, she asked:

"What are you going to show me this afternoon? And please do not say 'nothing' because I am greedy for that and want more!"

"I thought," the Earl said, "you would perhaps like to drive round some of the estate. Since we walked quite a long way this morning, we could leave the gardens for another time."

He thought for a moment before he went on:

"There are of course the stables also, and I think you will appreciate a Temple we have in the grounds which was designed by Vanbrugh in 1724 and is considered a gem of garden architecture."

He spoke somewhat pompously, but Noella gave a cry of delight and clapped her hands together.

"Of course I would love to see the Temple," she said, "and everything else you can show me. How lucky you are to possess anything so wonderful as this Castle and its surroundings."

"It is your home too!" the Earl said quietly.

Noella did not reply.

It suddenly struck her how wrong it was of her to deceive him.

She could see so clearly her own small black-and-white home sadly in need of being repainted.

The holes in the roof where the tiles had been blown off and the many diamond-paned windows cracked and broken beyond repair.

She thought too of the wild, overgrown garden which in the last years had become almost like a jungle.

"That is where I belong," she told herself.

Deep in her thoughts she did not realise that the Earl was watching her and suddenly he asked:

"What is upsetting you?"

"N . . nothing," Noella replied quickly.

"That is not true! When you first came here you were apprehensive. That is understandable, but now something else is worrying you, and I want you to tell me what it is."

With an effort Noella forced a smile to her lips.

"The only thing that is really worrying me," she said, "is that I shall wake up to find this has all been a dream!"

She thought it was rather a quick reply on the spur of the moment.

Yet she knew as the Earl rose to leave the table that he did not believe her.

When they came back from their drive in an open Phaeton drawn by two superb horses, the dressmaker was waiting.

It was the Butler who informed the Earl:

"She arrived half-an-hour ago, M'Lord, and she's waiting for Her Ladyship in her bedroom."

"Now you can choose your trousseau," the Earl said.

Remembering what he had said about being married, Noella shuddered at the word.

Then she said impulsively:

"Please, will you help me decide what I should have? I am afraid of buying the wrong things when I have not had a chance for so long, to buy myself even a pocket-handkerchief."

For a moment the Earl seemed surprised. Then he said:

"Very well. Put on what the dressmaker has brought for you, and then come and show me what you are wearing. I will be in the Library."

Noella gave him a little smile and ran up the stairs.

She found Nanny talking to the dressmaker, a middle-aged woman who had brought with her two attendants.

She must also have brought most of her stock.

The bedroom was piled with dress-boxes, some of which had been unpacked and their contents laid out on the bed or hanging on the wardrobe.

There was so much that for the moment Noella felt afraid.

Then as she thought of the gowns she had been wearing

which were all threadbare, and which were all she possessed, she began to feel elated.

First she was helped into day-dresses which with their tight waists, large sleeves and full skirts were very becoming.

As soon as she was dressed in one she ran downstairs to where the Earl was waiting.

He did not rise from his desk, but merely looked up as she came into the room.

Because it was so exciting to have a full-skirted gown after the old-fashioned ones that were long and slim, Noella swung round to show him how the skirt could move gracefully as she did so.

Then she waited, her eyes on his face.

"Yes, have it!" he said and looked down again at the letter he was reading.

She fled upstairs and three more day-dresses were set on one side before the evening-gowns were lifted from their boxes.

To Noella they were so lovely that she felt when she put on the first one which had frills covered with diamanté, like a Princess in a Fairy-Tale.

Now she walked down the stairs rather more sedately, enjoying the 'swish' of silk as she moved.

She was aware that above the low décolletage her skin looked very white.

She thought as she looked at her reflection in the mirrors as she passed them, that she looked like a flower.

She walked into the Library and because she thought it appropriate, she dropped the Earl a deep curtsy.

Then she stood in front of his desk awaiting his verdict.

He looked up at her, and to her surprise his eyes hardened.

"The neck is too low," he said sharply, "and the bodice too revealing. Tell the dressmaker if she has not something more ladylike to offer you she can take herself and her garments back to York!"

The way he spoke made Noella feel as if he had slapped her in the face.

For a moment she could not move, but could only stand looking at him, and because she was tired and his reaction was so unexpected, tears came into her eyes.

As she would have turned towards the door his fist came down sharply on the desk.

"I want my sister to look a Lady," he said angrily, "not like a – play-actress!"

There was a pause before he said the last word and Noella suspected he was about to say 'like a scarlet woman', and was thinking of his mother.

She went upstairs slowly.

It was with difficulty that she found amongst the dressmaker's evening gowns one that was more simple and gained the Earl's approval.

He passed two others, then he sent for the dressmaker.

Noella was not present when he spoke to the woman, but she had the idea that he had made if very clear exactly what he wanted.

After that, several other gowns were not even unpacked.

She was however allowed to choose her own night-gowns and under-clothes.

As they were all ornamented with real lace and made of the finest silk she had the feeling that the Earl would certainly have disapproved of them.

She accepted the dressmaker's suggestion that she should have a number of other accessories to be sent to her as soon as possible.

The dressmaker was certainly satisfied as she left.

After a rest, Noella put on one of the gowns of which the Earl had approved, she was still afraid that he might change his mind and become incensed.

It was the fashion in evening-gowns for the bodice to be very tight and the neckline above it to reveal the top of the wearer's shoulders.

Noella tugged the bodice up as high as she could, but she could not alter the way it was cut.

She thought a little despairingly that her expanse of neck and chest looked very naked.

As she had never been to any evening parties, she only knew of fashions from *The Ladies Magazine* which her mother had borrowed from the Vicar's wife.

She therefore had no idea whether she was being outrageous or just in fashion.

She glared at herself in the mirror and it was Nanny who came to her rescue.

"What you wants with that gown, Miss Noella, is a necklace."

"If I had ever possessed one, it would have been sold ages ago!" Noella smiled.

"Nevertheless, I've got an idea," Nanny said.

There were some flowers in a vase on Noella's dressing-table.

Nanny was very able with her fingers, and skilfully she made a necklace out of them.

It was in the manner of the daisy-chain which Noella had made for her mother when she was a child.

Made of small blossoms and fastened around Noella's long neck, it made all the difference to the gown.

"Nanny, you are a genius!" Noella exclaimed. "If we had a shop we could sell your necklaces and make a fortune!"

Nanny looked gratified, then she said:

"As long as we're here, we don't need a shop!"

"Hush!" Noella warned looking nervously at the door.

'It's all right," Nanny replied. "They keeps saying in the Servants' Hall as how you looks exactly like you were before your mother took you away."

"I am so frightened of making a mistake," Noella murmured.

She had already told Nanny how she had explained to the Earl how kind she and Hawkins had been to her when Caroline and her mother had died.

"It is true, what I said!" Noella murmured as if she wanted to convince herself. "You were very kind to Noely, and you have looked after me ever since I was born."

"Well, let's hope somebody's looking after us all now," Nanny remarked, "otherwise we'll find ourselves back at home without a penny to our names!"

Noella gave a little shiver.

"Do you think that is what he will do if he finds out?"

"I'm sure of it!" Nanny said. "Make no mistake, Miss Noella, he's a hard man, and there's nobody says any different!"

Chapter Five

Riding back to the Castle, Noella thought she had never enjoyed herself as much as she had these last few days.

The Earl had not only taken her driving so that she could see the estate, he had also invited her to ride with him.

She had been pleased to find that although she had not been able to ride for nearly five years, she had not forgotten how to do so.

She had, in fact, been a very good rider when her father was still alive.

But when they grew poorer and after his death first one of the horses was sold, then another, eventually the stables were empty.

Now on the Earl's well-bred and well-trained horses she thought nothing could be more exciting and that included the presence of her escort.

She had admitted to herself when alone in her bedroom that she now really liked the Earl although she was still frightened of him because he was so unpredictable.

Some days he would be charming to her, talking interestingly of things she wanted to know, and appearing to enjoy her company.

Then, quite unexpectedly, he would be sullen and disagreeable, eyeing her suspiciously.

When he did this, she felt her heart thumping in case he had found out that she was deceiving him.

However she convinced herself it was because he was suspicious not only of her, but of all women.

She knew also perceptively that he was waiting for her to reveal something improper or unpleasant she had learnt when she was with her mother and Captain Fairburn.

What this could be she had no idea.

She was actually so ignorant of the places in which Noely had stayed that she could not really understand what the Earl expected.

She was aware because Noely had told her, that the Casinos in Venice were notorious.

They were part of the Festivals which took place every month in what was the most pleasure-loving city of the world.

She fortunately did not know that every Venetian Lady had a Cicero who was a kind of Squire or lover, even though they might not actually make love to each other.

The Venetian Gentlemen had what the English called 'other interests', which involved any of the beautiful women in the City other than their own wives.

If she had known that these ideas were passing through the Earl's mind, she would in fact, have been not so much horrified as surprised.

Because she had always lived in the country, Noella was very innocent.

Noelly had told her that in Paris the women were bedecked with jewels and parties were given for them which could be described as 'Orgies'.

Yet she did not realise there was anything particularly wicked about them.

The same applied to Rome.

Noely had chatted away about the compliments she had been paid by the dark-eyed Italians with whom Captain Fairburn gambled.

She had said:

"They rather frightened me, and when they called to see Mama, I used to run away and hide in case they tried to make love to me."

"Why should they do that?" Noella had asked open-eyed.

Then as if she had found the explanation for herself she said:

"Oh, I suppose they wanted to marry you!"

Noely had looked away, and there had been a faint flush in her cheeks as she had said:

"Italians have arranged marriages, which take place when they are very young."

"Are you saying that they were .. married men who were .. pursuing you?" Noella asked in a shocked voice.

Noely had hesitated before answering, then made up her mind it would be a mistake.

"Let us talk about something else," she said. "Thank goodness, I have left Venice, Rome, Naples, Paris and all those places for ever! And wherever Mama may want to go, I would much rather live here with you!"

Noella had been delighted.

They had walked into the garden to talk of what she considered were much more interesting subjects than men.

Now she was quite certain that the Earl was watching her in case she should behave in what he would consider an unladylike manner.

She was also very careful not to say anything which might make him ask her awkward questions which she could not answer.

Worse still, he might still think she was contaminated by what he referred to as 'the gutters of Europe'.

She had learnt a great deal more about him from Nanny than she could learn for herself.

Nanny of course had got her information from the servants in the Castle, most of whom were growing old and had been there when he was a little boy.

She would lie awake at night wondering how Cousin Caroline could have been so cruel as to leave him behind.

"Why did she not take him with her as well as Noely?" she would ask herself.

Then she knew the answer.

If her cousin had done so, the Earl would undoubtedly

have followed her and taken away both of the children.

He would never have allowed his son and heir to be brought up by another man, or educated in a foreign country.

It all seemed very complicated.

Yet she could not help thinking that Cousin Caroline who had arrived penniless at her home, must sometimes have regretted leaving the comfort of the Castle, even apart from its grandeur.

Every day Noella was more and more thrilled with the treasures it contained, and the marvellous buildings there were in the grounds.

The Temple of the Four Winds which the Earl had shown her was not the only one of his possessions that intrigued and delighted her.

There was a Mausoleum which had a magnificent carved interior of stone, and a stone fountain from which the water cascaded through a globe supported by Atlas.

It was so unusual and so magnificent that Noella felt herself spellbound by it.

The Earl smiled and said that she might have posed for one of the stone figures.

As he spoke in the dry manner she had learned to expect from him, she did not realise at first that it was intended as a compliment.

There were so many other treasures to see that Noella was afraid of missing something vital.

At the back of her mind there was always the fear that one day her deception would be exposed and she would be sent away from the Castle in disgrace.

She thought if that happened it would be like being shut out of Paradise, but she did not say so to the Earl.

She looked at him apprehensively until once again he asked:

"What is worrying you?"

"I think . . really," she replied lightly, "I am afraid I am dreaming and I shall wake up to find that the Castle has . . vanished and with it the fountain, the Temple and the . . garden itself!"

"And what about its owner?" he enquired.

She looked at him, thinking how handsome he looked astride a large black stallion, and said:

"I must admit you do not seem to me . . quite real!"

He smiled before he replied:

"Then what am I?"

"Perhaps a god from Olympus," she replied, "and just as unpredictable."

She spoke without thinking and the Earl asked:

"What do you mean by that?"

She thought she had made a mistake but it would be best to explain truthfully.

"I have always read," she said, "that the gods, from Zeus downwards, were unpredictably changeable in their likes and dislikes, and certainly in their attitude to human beings."

"You think that is what I am?"

She felt their conversation was getting too personal and after a little pause she said:

"Sometimes you are . . very kind to me . . at other times . . frightening!"

They rode on for a short distance until the Earl said:

"You are very different, Noella, from what I expected!"

Noella turned to look at him in surprise before she asked a little tentatively:

"What did you . . expect?"

"Somebody very sophisticated who would find it hard after living a cosmopolitan life in Europe to enjoy English country ways."

Noella sighed.

It was impossible for her to explain to him that she had never known any other kind of life.

As far as she was concerned, nothing could be more exciting than the way she was living now.

She thought the Earl was waiting for a reply and after a moment she said:

"I hope that what you are saying means that you are pleased with me, because I .. want to .. please you."

She urged her horse forward as she spoke.

By the time the Earl caught up with her she hoped he had forgotten what they had been talking about.

Every day she found herself waking with a feeling of excited anticipation of what she would be doing.

She had also begun to feel full of energy and she knew this was because she was eating delicious food four times a day.

There was no doubt too that Nanny and Hawkins felt the same.

They looked younger and they were obviously happy.

When Nanny dressed her in the morning, they could talk without being overheard.

It was then she soothed away Noella's fears of discovery by saying how everybody in the Castle admired her.

"They think you're even more beautiful than the Countess," Nanny said, "and that's not surprising, considerin' I always thought your mother was a good deal lovelier than 'Mrs. Fairburn', as she called herself!"

"It was fortunate that Noely and I looked so alike," Noella said in a low voice.

"If you asks me," Nanny said, "God was lookin' after us when He brought us here! If we'd stayed where we were much longer, we'd all have been in our coffins by now!"

She spoke with such certainty that Noella found it impossible to argue.

She knew as she rode with the Earl in the sunshine that the memory of how hungry and desperate she had felt because there was no money, was gradually fading from her mind.

Then as the Castle loomed ahead of them she said almost to herself:

"Could anything be more beautiful?"

"That is what I think every time I see it!" the Earl

replied, "and I cannot understand how anybody would want to leave it."

Knowing that he was referring to his mother, Noella said quickly:

"Well, I certainly wish never to go away, but to stay here for ever and ever!"

"Naturally that is impossible!" the Earl replied.

Noella turned to look at him in astonishment.

"Impossible? Why?"

"Because you will get married," he said.

Noella gave a little sigh of relief because for one awful moment she thought he was sending her away for other reasons.

"There is no hurry for that," she said lightly, after a little pause, "and if nobody asks me I shall be quite happy to remain here an 'old maid'!"

They had reached the front of the house by this time.

As the grooms waiting for them came hurrying to their horses' heads, the Earl dismounted, then lifted Noella to the ground.

She thought as he did so how strong he was, and how handsome.

In fact, it was impossible to believe that any man could be better-looking or smarter in his appearance.

They walked up the stone steps side by side, and as they reached the hall the Earl said:

"Hurry and change! Sir Stephen Horton is coming to luncheon."

"Again!" Noella exclaimed.

She thought the Earl had not heard as he handed his hat and riding-whip to one of the footmen.

She went up the stairs thinking it was disappointing that Sir Stephen Horton would make a third when she had hoped to have luncheon alone with the Earl.

In the last week there had been two or three small luncheon-parties at which the Earl had entertained his friends and his neighbours.

They had come to talk to him, Noella knew, about the

local race-meeting that was to take place the following month.

They also discussed horses about which the Earl was an expert.

Most of them were older men who had been surprised when they first met Noella, having no idea that the Earl had brought his sister back to the Castle.

When they left they had all said that their wives would want to meet Lady Noella and would be inviting her to their homes as soon as possible.

She learned however, that Sir Stephen Horton, who was slightly younger than the others, was unmarried.

He had appeared for the third time the day before yesterday, ostensibly to talk to the Earl about his brood mares.

Noella had found however, that he was paying quite an unexpected amount of attention to her personally.

There was something about him which she did not like.

This was apart from the fact that he was rather a bore and inclined to give a lecture on every possible subject, rather than discuss it.

"I hope he does not stay long," Noella said to herself as she walked along the corridor to her bedroom. "I want Lyndon to take me driving this afternoon."

Almost as much as riding, she enjoyed driving with the Earl in a comfortable Chaise without even a groom to overhear their conversation.

She liked to watch the way he controlled his horses never using his whip.

Yet he got a speed out of his team which she was sure was exceptional.

Now she thought crossly that Sir Stephen would drone on until perhaps late in the afternoon.

They would be obliged to listen to him, instead of being out in the sunshine.

She changed from her riding-habit into one of the pretty day-dresses which had come from York.

It had the very large sleeves which were fashionable and a full skirt.

With her tiny waist, which was still too thin after years of privation, Noella looked fragile and almost ethereal.

Her gown was the colour of the first forget-me-nots showing their tiny blue petals amongst the more flamboyant flowers in the garden.

She had no idea how beautiful she looked with her fair hair framing her small pointed face as she walked into the Drawing-Room.

"Oh, here you are, Noella!" the Earl exclaimed. "Sir Stephen was just enquiring what had happened to you."

"I am sorry if I have kept you waiting," Noella said.

She put her hand into Sir Stephen's as she spoke and knew he held it longer than was necessary.

Luncheon was announced and they all walked into the Dining-Room.

As Noella had expected, the conversation immediately centred round horses and it left her free to think about the pictures and the beauty of the painted ceiling.

She was so intent on her thoughts that she was quite surprised when luncheon came to an end.

As they moved to leave the room Sir Stephen said to the Earl:

"May I speak to you alone, Ravensdale?"

"Of course," the Earl agreed. "Come into the Library. I am sure Noella will find plenty to occupy her in the Music-Room."

"Of course!" Noella replied.

There had been little time to play the piano since she had arrived.

But whenever she went to the Music-Room she was thrilled by the classical round ceiling design, which was mirrored by that of the carpet.

There were large, decorative paintings by Zucchi on the walls, Chippendale gilt chairs and sofas with a flowery Beauvais tapestry, and carved gilt tables beneath the windows.

She sat down at the piano and started to play.

As she did so, she felt the room was filled with the men and women of an age now past.

They were dressed in the colourful clothes worn by Louis XVI and Marie Antoinette.

Noella was dreaming that they danced to the music she was playing when the door opened.

She came back from her dreams thinking that the Earl had come to find her to tell her that Sir Stephen had left.

Then as her fingers fell from the keyboard she saw Sir Stephen come into the room alone.

Because she was disappointed, she made no effort to rise from the piano-stool, but merely sat waiting as he walked across the room towards her.

"Your music is very romantic, Noella!" he said.

It was the first time he had addressed her so informally, and she replied, deliberately using his title:

"Are you musical, Sir Stephen?"

"No," he replied, "but for the moment I would like to be a poet."

"A poet?" Noella exclaimed.

She could not imagine anything less likely than that Sir Stephen Horton would *read* poetry, let alone compose it.

There was a little pause, then Noella asked:

"Is Lyndon waiting for . . me?"

"I want to speak to you," Sir Stephen answered.

She looked up at him and saw an expression in his eyes she did not understand.

Then he said:

"I have asked your brother for his permission to marry you, and he has given his consent."

Noella felt that she could not have heard him aright. With a little exclamation that was one of fear she rose to her feet.

"No, no! Of course . . not!" she said.

She would have moved away, but she was hemmed in by the music-stool and the piano, and Sir Stephen reached out to take her hand.

"I want you to be my wife," he said, "and I am sure, Noella, we will be very happy together."

As his fingers closed over hers, Noella felt as if he menaced her and she wanted to run away.

Since that was impossible, she tried to pull her hand away from his, but he held to it tightly, saying:

"My house may not be as magnificent as the Castle, but it has been in my family for two-hundred years, and you will certainly be the most beautiful of all the women who have been its chatelaine."

"I . . I am sorry," Noella said in a very small voice, "and while I am very . . honoured that you should wish to marry . . me . . Sir Stephen . . I . . I cannot do so."

Sir Stephen smiled.

"Because you are very young," he said, "I can understand that you are nervous, and perhaps a little frightened of marriage. But you will find me a kind and generous husband, and nowhere in England could there be a better place in which to rear our children than Yorkshire!"

Noella drew in her breath.

She had the feeling that he was not listening to what she said.

He seemed to be simply assuming that she would be his wife, whatever her feelings were in the matter.

With difficulty she managed to extract her hand from his, and clasping her fingers together, she said:

"Please . . listen to me."

"I am listening," Sir Stephen answered, "but I must tell you, Noella, that I will not take 'No' for an answer. Your brother has consented to our marriage, and I intend to send the announcement of our engagement to the newspapers within a few days."

"No!" Noella said again.

Now he reached forward and attempted to draw her into his arms.

She realised that he intended to kiss her, and fought herself free.

Before he could expostulate, before he could catch hold

of her, she ran across the room to escape down the passage.

She heard him call her name, but she did not stop.

All she wanted was to tear through the hall and up the great Grand Staircase to reach the security of her own bedroom.

She shut the door, turned the key in the lock and sank down on a chair for the moment breathless and very frightened.

"How could I have .. known .. how could I have .. guessed," she asked herself, "that the Earl .. intended to marry me off so .. quickly .. and to Sir Stephen Horton of all .. people!"

She knew when he touched her that the idea of being kissed by him was repulsive. Moreover apart from thinking him a pompous bore, she positively disliked him as a man.

"How could I marry someone like that?" she asked herself wildly.

She remembered the love her father and mother had had for each other: the happiness which had seemed to shine from them like an inner light.

She knew that was what she wanted, and it was certainly something she would never find with Sir Stephen Horton.

"I must make the Earl .. understand," she thought.

She sat for a long time in the chair, then rose to her feet to look at herself in the mirror.

It was impossible that she could look so ordinary, when a feeling of horror that was inexpressible was sweeping over her.

Suppose the Earl would not listen to her?

She found herself trembling.

Then because she felt helpless, she began to pray:

"Help me .. Mama .. help me!" she pleaded. "How can I marry any .. man unless I feel like .. you did .. about Papa?"

For the first time she understood that the love that she

hoped for was what Cousin Caroline must have felt for D'Arcy Fairburn.

Perhaps she too had been disillusioned, perhaps disgusted by the Earl!

Perhaps that was why she had been so brave as to run away with a man she could not marry.

It was wrong, it was wicked, Noella knew, but it was just as wrong to marry somebody she did not love, whose very touch made her shiver.

"I have to .. make the Earl .. understand!" she said again.

She wondered what was happening downstairs, and if Sir Stephen had reported her behaviour to her.

"Perhaps now he will not want to marry me!" she told herself optimistically.

Then she remembered the expression there had been in Sir Stephen's eyes, which she had never noticed before.

Because he had always seemed so dry and pompous, she had hardly thought of him as a human being.

Yet, when he clung to her hand, then attempted to put his arms around her, she had known he found her attractive as a woman.

"How .. can I .. bear it?" she asked aloud and thought her voice had a shrill note in it that was one of fear.

Finally, after over an hour had passed, she tidied her hair, and knowing her heart was beating tempestuously went slowly down the stairs.

She had almost reached the hall when the Butler coming into it from the corridor at the other end, exclaimed:

"I was just coming to look for your Ladyship. His Lordship wishes to speak to you."

"Is he .. alone?" Noella asked.

"Yes, M'Lady. Sir Stephen left a short while ago."

Slowly, as if every footstep was an effort, Noella walked down the broad corridor which led to the Library.

Now the statues on either side of it seemed, she thought, like jailors taking away her freedom.

She thought that Ceres mocked at her because she was

96

refusing the Cornucopia of Plenty she was being offered by a wealthy man.

"I would rather marry a beggar or a crossing-sweeper!" Noella told herself.

She lifted her chin as the Butler opened the Library door and walked in with her head held high.

The Earl was standing at the window looking out at the garden.

He turned round as she entered, and there was silence, as she moved slowly, very slowly towards him.

Because she was frightened she did not dare look at his face and she felt sure he was scowling.

As she reached him he said in what she thought was a harsh tone:

"As you already know, Sir Stephen Horton has asked for your hand, and I have given my consent to your marriage."

Noella opened her lips to speak, but he went on:

"I should have perhaps explained to you before that he is one of the richest men in the County. He owns a magnificent house and although he was married, he has been a widower for the last ten years."

"He . . he was . . m.married!"

It was difficult for Noella to say the words, but the Earl heard them.

"He was not, I understand, happy, but that need not concern you. I consider you very fortunate that a man of such substance and the head of an aristocratic family, should be prepared to accept you as his wife."

Noella drew in her breath.

"But I am . . not prepared to . . accept him!"

"Why not!"

The question sounded like a pistol-shot, and she replied:

"Because I . . I do not . . love him!"

"I have already told you that the love you talk about is of no importance, and in your case merely the romantic nonsense of an young girl's dream."

His voice hardened as he went on:

"It has no reality, in fact it is a mirage thought up by novelists in order to make money, and believed in only by nitwits!"

"That is . . not true!" Noella retorted. "It is the only . . possible foundation for a . . happy marriage."

She thought of her father and mother and forced herself to choose her words carefully as she said:

"I have known . . people who have been . . supremely and totally . . happy because they . . love each other . . even though they had . . no money."

"They were exceptional," the Earl sneered. "I have no intention of allowing you to accept the proposal of some fortune-hunter or a social climber who wished to be linked with our distinguished family."

"It is hardly a . . question where I am concerned . . of a man . . wanting me for my . . fortune," Noella said, thinking that this at least gave her a chance to argue.

"That is where you are mistaken," the Earl replied. "You have been left a considerable amount of money in our father's will, which you were only to receive if and when you chose to return home and take your rightful place as his daughter."

Noella was so surprised that she could only gape at the Earl.

"Y. you mean . . I have . . money of my . . own?"

"I had intended to tell you about it when you arrived," he replied, "but it escaped my memory until Sir Stephen, who was in my father's confidence, spoke of it just now."

Noella was so astonished that she could make no reply and the Earl went on:

"It is of course, of little consequence, as Sir Stephen is himself a very wealthy man."

"Even if he were as 'rich as Croesus' . . I would not . . marry him!"

"That is where you are mistaken," the Earl retorted. "You are obliged to marry whomsoever as your Guardian, I might choose for you, and I think when you consider it sensibly, you will realise that Sir Stephen is exactly the right husband for you."

"I do not .. wish to .. marry him," Noella said, "He is not .. only a bore .. but I actively .. dislike him!"

"Nonsense!" the Earl exclaimed angrily. "And as he is older than you, he will look after you, protect you, and see that you do not make the sort of mistake that . . ."

He stopped, and Noella knew exactly what he was about to say.

For a moment she contemplated telling him that whatever had happened to his mother after her husband's death, she had been very much in love with the man with whom she had run away.

Her mother had, in fact, told her:

"Caroline was saying to me last night that poor though she is now, if she had to make the choice all over again of staying with her husband or running away with D'Arcy Fairburn, she could not hesitate."

Noella had known when her mother spoke that she was surprised that her cousin could still feel like that.

Yet because she had loved her own husband so dearly she had understood.

Now remembering her mother's stand, Noella faced the Earl all the more defiantly.

"It is no .. use, whatever .. you may say .. nothing will make me .. marry Sir Stephen Horton!"

"You will marry him, if I have to drag you to the altar!" the Earl replied angrily. "Do you not understand, you stupid, idiotic child, that I am doing what is best for you? I am quite certain in view of the circumstances in which you have lived these last sixteen years, you will never have a better offer."

"I do not .. want a better .. offer!" Noella cried. "If I marry .. and there is no hurry .. I will marry only .. a man .. I love!"

"You will marry whom I tell you to!" the Earl exploded.

"I will not .. and you cannot .. make me, and if you try .. I shall .. run away!"

The last two words, and the way she spoke them, made the Earl lose his self-control.

To her astonishment he reached out and taking her by the shoulders shook her.

"How dare you defy me!" he raged. "You are as bad as your mother! I will not tolerate it from you, even if I have to beat you into submission!"

He was shaking her as he spoke, shaking her backwards and forwards, as if she was a rag-doll.

It made her feel dizzy and breathless but at the same time, she was determined not to give in to him.

"I hate .. him! I will .. not marry .. him!" she gasped until the Earl shook the words from her lips.

Then he stopped and looked at her with an expression of fury on his face.

Her hair had become loose and was flowing over her shoulders; her eyes defiant, yet at the same time dark with fear, could only stare at him.

Her lips trembled and her hands moved feebly against him as if trying to prevent him from hurting her.

For a moment they just looked at each other. Then the Earl said.

"Damn you! You will do as you are told, or I swear I will beat you!"

Because he spoke so furiously and for the first time his voice was raised so that it seemed to echo round the room, Noella felt the tears come into her eyes.

Though determined to go on defying the Earl, she could not help giving a little sob.

It was then he released his hold on her and walking across the room went out of the Library, slamming the door behind him.

Slowly, because she no longer had the strength to stand, Noella crumpled down onto the floor.

With the tears pouring down her cheeks, she hid her face in her hands.

Chapter Six

Noella reached her bedroom, having controlled her tears as she went through the hall.

She sat down in the same chair in which she had sat before and tried to compose herself.

She could hardly believe that the Earl, who had been so kind and charming during the morning, could suddenly have become so cruel and insensitive.

How could he force her to marry a man whom she actively disliked?

How could he shake her until she was dizzy and threaten that he would beat her if she did not obey him?

It all seemed incomprehensible and once again she found the tears running down her cheeks.

She wanted to be with her father and mother for comfort and most of all, to escape from the future.

"I will .. not marry him .. I will .. not!" she murmured.

She felt as if she was being enclosed in a prison from which she would never be free.

She must have been in her room for over an hour when the door opened and Nanny came in.

"What are you doing here, Miss Noella?" she asked. "I thought you'd be downstairs, and that's where the footmen are looking for you."

"What for?" Noella asked.

She had got up when Nanny entered and walked to the dressing-table so that she should not see she had been crying.

But perhaps her voice gave her away, for Nanny coming nearer asked:

"What's the matter, Dearie, what's upset you?"

Noella felt so upset that she could not speak of it and instead she enquired:

"Why are . . the footmen . . looking for . . me?"

"His Lordship's received bad news!"

"Bad news?" Noella questioned.

"I think he's written a note for you," Nanny said. "Wait a minute, while I go to get it."

Nanny went from the room and Noella wondered why he should have done so.

Then she thought despairingly that if indeed His Lordship had written her a note, it was doubtless to tell her that she was to marry Sir Stephen and make no more fuss about it.

"I hate them . . both!" she told her reflection in the mirror.

Then she knew that where the Earl was concerned that was not true.

She enjoyed being with him, she liked listening to him.

If she was honest, the reason why the Castle seemed enchanted was that she was there with him.

Now he had spoilt everything.

She wanted to storm at him that it was unfair, that he had no right to behave like a Sultan and give her orders which he expected her to obey.

Nanny was away for some time, and when she returned she came in saying:

"They was looking for you in the Music-Room. I had to go down the stairs and all along the passage to find them!"

She held out an envelope as she spoke.

Noella took it from her and saw her name written in the Earl's strong, upright handwriting.

She felt her heart begin to beat in a frightened fashion.

As she opened the envelope she was aware that her hands were trembling and for a moment what was written on the page seemed to dance in front of her eyes.

"Dear Noella,

I have just received the information that Uncle Robert, our father's younger brother, has died. He lived about twenty miles from here, and his wife has asked me to go to her immediately.

I cannot of course refuse, and I shall be away tonight, but will be returning tomorrow, as soon as I have arranged the Funeral.

As we will be in mourning, this means the question of your marriage must be postponed for the moment. I suggest therefore you do not upset yourself, and we will discuss the matter on my return.

I remain,
Your affectionate brother,
Lyndon."

Noella read what he had written, and it seemed as if the sunshine had suddenly come through the clouds.

She knew him well enough now to know that what he had said about her marriage was, in a way, an apology.

Now she had the hope that he would be more reasonable.

Perhaps she could make him agree that, although she was prepared to marry sometime, it need not be to Sir Stephen, however eligible he might be.

She read the letter through again, then asked in a very different voice from the one she had used before:

"Has His Lordship . . left?"

"About half-an-hour ago," Nanny replied. "I believe he asked for you, but when you couldn't be found, he drove off."

Noella gave a little sigh of relief.

She knew she had been afraid of having to see the Earl that evening and continuing their dispute.

Now she was free at least until tomorrow, and then until they were no longer in mourning.

"His Lordship informs me," Noella said to Nanny, "that his Uncle Robert has died."

"Mr. Johnson told me that before I came upstairs," Nanny replied. "He was a sick man, but apparently they was all fond of him."

"How long do we have to be in mourning for him?" Noella asked.

It was an important question as far as she was concerned and she waited apprehensively for Nanny's reply.

"I should think about four to six months'd be correct," Nanny answered, "but you'll have to ask His Lordship. People has different ideas about mourning."

"That will certainly be a respite," Noella thought.

"You'll have to have a black dress for the Funeral, Nanny was saying, "and I should think after that you could wear just a black sash round your other gowns, and perhaps a black ribbon in your hair. It's not as if you'll be entertaining."

Noella did not reply.

She was thinking she would willingly wear black or even sack-cloth, so long as she did not have to marry Sir Stephen.

It was the best thing that could ever have happened that her supposed uncle should have died so conveniently.

Nanny was chattering on:

"You'll not want to dine downstairs in the big Drawing-Room all alone and Mr. Johnson's already suggested you should have your dinner in the Boudoir."

Noella knew that the Boudoir adjoined her room.

But as there were so many other rooms to inspect, and downstairs she could be with the Earl, she had actually only peeped inside it.

Now Nanny opened the communicating door and she saw that it was in fact, a very pretty room.

There were gold framed mirrors on the brocaded walls, and elegant French furniture which complemented the

Dresden china which decorated the mantelpiece.

"I shall be quite happy in here," Noella said to Nanny with a smile, "and happier still if you could have dinner with me!"

"That'd certainly shock them below-stairs!" Nanny replied. "I'm expected to 'keep my place', and that's what I intends to do!"

Noella put her arms around Nanny's shoulders and kissed her cheek.

"Your place is with me," she said. "You are all I have left of the old days when we were so happy."

There was a little sob in her voice which made Nanny say hastily:

"Now, don't you go upsetting yourself. We're very lucky to be here with a roof over our heads that don't leak, and plenty of food in our tummies!"

Noella laughed because it was so like Nanny to talk with so much common sense.

Because she wanted to take her mind off the altercation she had had with the Earl, she sat down to read a book until her dinner was brought upstairs.

Waited on by two footmen, she enjoyed a delicious meal and only wished that her mother could see her in such grand surroundings.

When she had finished and the footmen had withdrawn, she was considering whether she should go to bed.

There was a knock on the door and one of the footmen came back into the room with a note on a silver tray.

"This has been left for you, M'Lady."

"By whom?" Noella enquired.

"I don't know, M'Lady."

When the footman had left Noella looked at the note which bore her name and felt sure it was from Sir Stephen.

There was no one else, she thought, who was likely to write to her.

Although there had been two invitations from wives of the Earl's friends, they had written to Lyndon and not directly to her.

For a moment she contemplated throwing the letter into the fire.

Then she told herself she had to behave sensibly.

Moreover it would be a mistake to antagonise the Earl and make him angry again.

She opened the note, then stared at it in astonishment.

There was only one sentence in the centre of the writing-paper.

"Meet me as soon as possible in the Temple of the Four Winds!"

She stared at it, thinking that it must be meant for somebody else.

Then she understood.

The note was not from Sir Stephen, as she had feared, but from Jasper Raven!

She had seen his hand-writing when they had stayed in London on the journey North.

There was no mistaking the way he formed some of his capitals, which was different from the way she wrote them herself.

Then with a little throb of fear, she wondered what Jasper wanted with her.

She thought when the Earl had sent him away she was never likely to see him again.

Yet now she knew what he had written was a command that she dared not disobey.

She rose to look out of the window.

It was dusk. Already the first evening star was shining faintly in the sky and she knew that later there would be a moon.

"I suppose I shall have to go to him," she thought.

She was afraid that if she did not do so, he might come to the Castle and demand to see her.

She went into her bedroom next door and found an attractive Paisley shawl to wear over her gown.

She knew that Nanny would be downstairs having supper with the rest of the staff.

The only servant who would be in that part of the Castle was the footman on duty in the hall.

She therefore went from her bedroom and down a side-staircase which led her to a door opening into the garden which she had used before.

Although the shadows were long and the trees were dark, it was easy to find her way across the green lawn.

She passed the magnificent fountain which was still throwing its water up into the sky, and came to the Temple of the Four Winds.

It was a domed building with four Ionic porticoes, and splendidly carved finials.

The interior was enriched with white and gilded plaster.

The walls were in veined white and the columns and architraves in black and gold, and were very impressive.

Noella however was conscious only of the man she sensed was waiting for her even before she saw him.

He came from behind a pillar and the evening light through the open window made him seem sinister.

It was only with a tremendous effort of self-control that she did not run away.

"Good evening, Noella!" Jasper said.

"Why do you . . want to . . see me?" Noella asked in a low voice. "Surely . . it is a . . mistake?"

"I have been waiting for my kind, generous cousin to leave you alone," Jasper replied, "and when I learnt that he had left the Castle for the night, I knew this was my opportunity."

It flashed through Noella's mind that he must have a spy to tell him of the Earl's movements.

She did not reply to what he had said, and after a moment he walked to one of the open windows.

Because she felt there was nothing else she could do, she followed him.

He did not speak, and after a moment she asked:

"Why . . did you . . want to . . see me?"

"I want your help."

"My . . help?"

"It is quite simple," Jasper replied. "Your so-called brother has fobbed me off with a pittance, and I therefore intend to take what I am entitled to – without his permission!"

Noella gave a little gasp.

"You cannot . . mean you are . . going to . . steal something from . . the Castle?"

"I intend to steal a great deal," Jasper replied, "and that is where you are going to help me."

"No . . of course not . . how could I do . . such a thing?"

"Very easily," Jasper said with a twist of his lips, "unless you want to be exposed for the liar you are."

Noella gave a little cry.

"Are you . . threatening . . me?"

"Of course I am," Jasper replied, "and let me point out, my pretty little deceiver, there is nothing you can do about it, unless you want yourself and those tiresome old servants you make such a fuss about to be thrown out and left to starve!"

He spoke in a way which made Noella know that he was enjoying frightening her, and she said:

"How can . . you be so . . despicable? How can you . . expect me to . . help you . . steal from somebody who has shown . . me nothing but . . kindness?"

Jasper laughed.

"Very easily," he said. "You of all people should know how uncomfortable it is to be without money, and I therefore want something to sell. There is a great deal that will not be missed."

"Of course it will be missed!" Noella insisted. "The Earl knows . . everything he possesses, and even if you take the very smallest ornament, one of the servants will be . . aware that it is . . missing."

"When it is gone, what can Lyndon do about it?" Jasper enquired. "And I cannot believe, seeing how deeply involved you are, that you are likely to explain its absence."

He seemed to be speaking as if with a poisoned tongue.

Then suddenly Noella gave a little cry.

"I have just thought of something," she said. "There is no need for you to steal! I can help you!"

"How is that possible?" Jasper enquired.

"The Earl told me this afternoon that his father left a considerable sum of money to his daughter 'if and when' she returned home."

For a moment Jasper was silent. Then he said:

"That is certainly something I did not expect, and I should of course, be very grateful for anything you condescend to give me, once the money is in your hands."

"I promise I will give you anything I can," Noella said, thinking he had accepted her suggestion.

"I am not a fool," Jasper sneered. "The money will be in trust, and you will only be allowed a small amount with which to dress yourself. As far as I am concerned, that will be only a 'drop in the ocean'."

Noella drew in her breath but did not speak, and he continued:

"What I am talking about is real money! I need it at once, and that is what I intend to have!"

"But .. you must not .. steal it!" she pleaded. "I cannot .. help you!"

"You have to," he said firmly. "All you have to do is let me in to the Castle through the garden door, which is doubtless the one you used tonight, and lock it again when I have left."

Noella felt herself tremble.

"Why must I do that?"

"It will be better for me," Jasper replied, "to be a long way from the Castle when the so-called 'burglary' is discovered."

"It is wrong .. I know it is .. wrong!" Noella murmured.

"Stop arguing, and just do as I tell you!" Jasper said savagely. "When is Lyndon expected to return?"

"He said he would be . . back some time tomorrow . . after he has arranged the Funeral."

"Funeral? What Funeral?"

"His Uncle Robert has died."

She was then aware that Jasper was staring at her almost incredulously.

"Are you quite sure that it is the Honourable Robert Raven who has died?" he asked after a moment.

"Lyndon said it was his father's younger brother."

To her astonishment Jasper gave what was almost a cry of delight.

"Robert Raven dead!" he said in a tone of apparent satisfaction. "I never expected that! I thought he would linger on for years!"

"But why? How does it affect you?" Noella asked.

"Of course it affects me, you stupid fool!'

"But . . how? I do not . . understand."

Jasper opened his mouth to speak, then changed his mind and said instead:

"There is no need for you to ask questions and all you have to do is exactly what I tell you. Tomorrow . . ."

"Tomorrow!" Noella exclaimed. "I thought you would be coming to the Castle tonight! Surely it would be safer . . if you . . insist on . . stealing something . . to come when Lyndon is . . away!"

"That is what I had intended," Jasper said, "but now I have changed my mind. I want the Earl to be there – in fact it is very important that he should be!"

He was speaking in the same sinister voice which had frightened her before.

She only wished she could see him a little more clearly, which might make it easier for her to guess what he was thinking.

Then, as if he made up his mind, he said;

"Now listen, and make no mistakes! if you do not do as I tell you, I will expose you and knowing only too well what my dear cousin feels about the deceit and treachery of women, I warn you that you will be out on your ear without a penny in your pocket!"

Because he seemed to spit the words at her, Noella gave a little cry of protest, and Jasper went on:

"I am sure you will enjoy seeing that old crone you call 'Nanny' dying in front of your eyes, although perhaps your father's man-servant may be able to survive."

"You are .. not to say .. such things to .. me!"

"Of course," Jasper went on, "seeing how pretty you are, you will doubtless find some man to offer you his protection, but it will certainly not include a wedding-ring!"

Noella realised he was deliberately insulting her, and because she felt the humiliation of it, she said quickly:

"I have .. said I .. will do what .. you want."

"Do it, and do it properly!" Jasper said.

"But I think you should come tonight," Noella insisted. "The door is open and, if you follow me to the Castle, I can go to my room and know nothing of what happens."

"That will be very nice and convenient for you, will it not?" Jasper said mockingly.

It was now almost dark, but she had a feeling that he was looking at her in a strange way, appraising her, but she did not know why.

Then unexpectedly he gave an exclamation.

"What is it?" she asked.

"I have cut my finger," he replied. "Give me your handkerchief."

Noella felt in the sash around her waist and found one which Nanny had given her before dinner.

As she pulled it out, she realised it was one of the few things which she owned herself and had not been bought with the Earl's money.

It was a handkerchief her mother had made for her as a Christmas present, and was embroidered with her initials at the corner surrounded by flowers.

She hesitated then as Jasper was holding his hand higher than the window-sill she exclaimed:

"You have a handkerchief of your own! I can see it tucked into your cuff!"

"Give me yours!" he said harshly.

Without waiting for her to do so, he snatched it from her hand and twisted it round one of his fingers.

She thought it was exceedingly rude, but there was no point in saying so.

"Now listen to what I have to say and make no mistakes," he said. "After Lyndon has retired tomorrow night – and make sure sure he has gone upstairs and is in his room – unlock the garden-door."

He spoke slowly as if he was thinking it out as he went on:

"I shall be waiting outside and if the stairs are unlit, you can guide me until we reach the corridor where you are sleeping, and where my generous cousin is in the Master Suite."

Again he was speaking in the horrible, spiteful way he had done before, and Noella shivered.

"Go back," Jasper said sharply, "and be sure you are not seen. If you are, and anybody asks you where you have been, say you have been outside for a breath of fresh air. Do you understand?"

"Yes . . of course," Noella replied dully.

"Then go! What are you waiting for? And do not let me down tomorrow night, or you will be very sorry you have done so!"

Again he was threatening her and because she could not bear to hear any more Noella turned away as quickly as she could.

She moved through the darkness inside the Temple and stepped out with a feeling of relief.

Now the stars filled the sky, and it was easy to see the great Castle with its turrets and towers ahead of her.

As she hurried over the green lawns towards it she felt every footstep was carrying her away from the horror of Jasper.

He was like a poisonous snake, she thought, and she

found it difficult to think of anything except that she hated him.

She entered the Castle by the garden-door, bolted and locked it as it had been before she went outside, and hurried up the stairs to her bedroom.

Nanny was waiting for her and asked as she came into the room:

"Where have you been?"

"Downstairs," Noella replied.

"I thought you'd be in the Library looking at books!" Nanny said.

Noella did not contradict her and she went on:

"Now just you get into bed, and go to sleep. It'll do you good to have a rest – and no reading! You'll be blind by the time you're my age at this rate!"

It was something Noella had heard before and somehow it was comforting because it was so familiar.

She let Nanny help her undress.

Only when the old woman was blowing out the light did she long to tell her what had happened, and ask her what she should do.

Then she knew it would only distress Nanny and give her a sleepless night, and that would be unkind.

"Goodnight, Nanny," she said, "and remember me in your prayers."

"I always do that," Nanny replied, "and I feel sure when you are praying your dear mother hears it, an' if anyone was a saint on earth, it was her!"

When Nanny shut the door and she was alone, Noella tried to pray to her mother.

"Help me . . Mama . . help me! I know what I am doing is . . wrong, and now Jasper will steal some precious . . treasures from the Castle and there will be a . . terrible scene about it, and . . perhaps I shall be . . involved."

She felt herself tremble at the idea.

Then as she prayed over and over again for help it was a long time before she fell asleep.

*

When morning came it seemed that her meeting with Jasper was like a nightmare and she could not believe it had really happened.

Then Nanny asked:

"Where's the handkerchief I gave you yesterday?"

Noella remembered all too vividly that Jasper had taken it.

"He even had to steal my handkerchief, rather than use his own," she wanted to reply, but knew she could not do so.

When she went downstairs she found herself looking in the various Reception Rooms and trying to determine what he was likely to take away.

Perhaps it would be the exquisite Famille Rose pots which she knew were priceless with their green and gold stands, or the ornaments of jade and crystal which the Earl had told her were also priceless.

In another Reception-Room there was a cabinet filled with snuff-boxes.

Many of them were covered with diamonds and other precious stones which she learned, made it a unique collection.

It was when she looked at the pictures and the miniatures that she wanted to cry out at the idea of their being taken away.

They were all part of the history of the Raven family.

It seemed so wrong and sordid that a collection formed over many generations should be spoilt by one spendthrift member of the family, who dissipated everything he was given.

"It is going to be very difficult for me," Noella thought, "when the burglary is discovered."

She knew she would have to be very careful not to become involved.

Because she was so worried and perturbed by what she had to do, she wandered around the Castle all day.

She moved from room to room, touching the china and the other ornaments as if she caressed them.

114

She looked at the pictures, afraid that when she next looked there the frames would be empty.

The Earl did not return until shortly before dinner.

She was downstairs waiting before him in the Drawing-Room where they usually met at seven-thirty.

He came into the room looking extremely elegant in his evening-clothes.

He was wearing long black drain-pipe trousers which had been introduced by George IV and which Noella thought were more attractive than knee-breeches and silk stockings.

"I apologise for being away so long, Noella," he said as he advanced towards her, "but there was far more for me to do than I expected."

"I am sorry to hear about your uncle's death," Noella said.

"*Our* uncle!" the Earl corrected, but he was smiling.

Then he went on;

"He did not suffer, which is a great thing, and his second wife, who is a very sensible woman, has behaved with a self-composure and dignity which made everything very much easier than it might have been."

"Had he any children?" Noella asked.

"Four daughters!" the Earl replied. "Which was of course, a great disappointment!"

As the Earl spoke he accepted a glass of champagne which Johnson proffered him, and sipped it as he said:

"What have you been doing with yourself all day?"

"Nothing very much," Noella replied, "I was just waiting for you to return."

"You look a little worried," the Earl said unexpectedly. "As I told you in my note, there is no need for you to get upset, at least not for the next six months."

Noella's heart gave a leap of joy, and she had no idea that her eyes were shining as she said:

"Thank you .. that makes me .. very much .. happier!"

The Earl looked at her, then walked towards the fireplace saying as he did so:

"The Funeral is not until next Saturday, and there is no need for you to attend, so let us talk of something more interesting."

"That is what I would . . like to . . do."

They talked all through dinner.

She knew that the Earl was trying to entertain her and being more charming than she had ever known him.

It was only when dinner was over and they had sat for a little while in the Drawing-Room in front of the fire that she began to grow apprehensive.

"I think we should go to bed," the Earl said. "Quite frankly I am tired since I sat up very late last night looking into Uncle Robert's affairs."

"Then I am sure you will sleep well," Noella said with a little tremor in her voice.

She thought the Earl looked at her questioningly, but he did not speak.

They walked together towards the door.

There were two footmen on duty in the hall.

As Noella went up the stairs she was aware that they were already beginning to put out the lights in the silver sconces and extinguish the candles in the chandeliers.

She and the Earl walked along the corridor which led to all the State Rooms in the main block, and when they reached Noella's room he asked:

"Shall we ride immediately after breakfast? I missed our ride this morning."

"So did I."

She looked up into his eyes as she spoke and somehow it was hard to look away.

Then almost abruptly he said: "Goodnight, Noella!" and walked down the passage towards his own Suite which was at the far end.

As she went into her bedroom where Nanny was waiting, Noella thought there was a warmth within her because the Earl had been so pleasant.

116

It was only when she was undressed that she shivered at the thought of what she had to do.

Nanny seemed to potter about for a long time, tidying away her clothes, and Noella wished she would leave her.

She wanted to think; she wanted to prepare herself.

"They was talking about Mr. Robert downstairs," Nanny was saying, "an' they all said what a nice gentleman he was."

Noella did not answer, and she went on:

"It's sad that with two wives he's never had a son. Of course, with His Lordship young enough to have a dozen of his own, there's no real need for it."

As she blew out the candles on the dressing-table she asked:

"And what do you think Mr. Johnson told me?"

With an effort Noella made herself realise that Nanny had asked her a question.

"What did he tell you?"

"He says as how if His Lordship doesn't have a son, Mr. Jasper, whom I wouldn't trust further than I could throw him, will now be the next Earl!"

When Nanny said Jasper's name, Noella felt herself start.

She knew that already he would be outside the Castle walls, waiting for her to open the door and let him in.

She wondered if he would have an accomplice with him, or whether he would take everything away himself.

Then Nanny said:

"Goodnight, Miss Noella, and sleep well."

"Goodnight, Nanny dear," Noella replied. "Call me at eight o'clock."

"I'll do that," Nanny answered and shut the door.

Noella made herself wait until she was quite certain Nanny had walked along the length of the corridor.

Then she would be climbing the stairs up to the second floor where she was sleeping.

Then she sat up in bed and lit one of the candles.

She got out of bed and put on the negligee that Nanny had left lying over the chair.

It was a very pretty one, rather more elaborate, she thought, than what her mother would have chosen for her.

Yet because it was something she had to decide for herself, she had been unable to resist it.

It was of blue silk, the colour of a summer sky, and the shadow lace which trimmed it she had believed when she was a child was made by fairy fingers.

"That will be for the summer," the Dressmaker from York had said, "but I will make Your Ladyship a velvet one for the winter and trim it with swan's-down."

Now, because she was frightened, Noella felt cold and she wished she had the velvet negligee to keep her warm.

Then as she slipped into her heelless slippers, she went to the window to look out at the sky.

As she had expected, the full moon was very bright and the garden outside seemed like a Fairyland.

Then as she thought of Jasper waiting on the other side of the Castle, she felt as if everything was in fact, dark and terrifying.

Very, very slowly, she opened her door.

As she expected, there were only two or three lights left burning in the corridor. The rest had been extinguished.

It was quite easy for her to see her way, walking on tip-toe to the top of the secondary staircase.

Everything was in darkness except that at the bottom where the garden-door was situated were some long windows which were uncurtained, reaching up to the ceiling.

She was therefore able to guide herself down the stairs by the light of the moon.

When she reached the door and knew that Jasper was waiting outside, she felt as if he was crouching there like some evil animal.

He would spring into the Castle and damage or destroy everything that was perfect about it.

As she reached the last step of the stairs she found herself wondering what would happen if the Earl was aware that it was she who had let the 'burglar' in.

Or if after she opened the door she found he was waiting in the corridor when she came up to return to her bedroom.

Again she wondered why Jasper had not come last night when the Earl was away.

She supposed it was because he had to arrange to have some accomplice with him to carry away his ill-gotten loot.

Then even as she pulled back the bolt on the door she knew the reason – the true reason – was like an explosion inside her.

Of course Jasper wanted the Earl to be in the Castle because now that he was his Heir Presumptive he intended to kill him!

It was such a shock that Noella felt stunned by the thoughts going round in her head.

Now it began to percolate into her mind and make her certain that what she was thinking was the truth.

Yet she was turning the key and pulling back the lower bolt.

It was then with a feeling, not only of incredulity, but of horror and disgust, that she turned and ran up the stairs, not waiting to see if Jasper came through the door she had left ajar.

She reached the landing.

Without thinking of anything except that she must save the Earl, she tore along the corridor to his room and pulled open the door.

Only as she realised it was not in total darkness, as she had expected, but the moonlight was coming through the open and uncurtained window, did she hesitate.

Then, with a little cry that was nothing more than a whisper, she ran to his bedside.

She could see the outline of his body beneath the blankets and she put out her hand to touch him on the shoulder saying as she did so:

"Lyndon! Lyndon! Wake up!"

"What – is it? What do you – want?"

Then he was awake with the quickness of a man used to being on the alert and she said in a voice he could hardly hear:

"It is . . Jasper!"

"Jasper?" the Earl asked in surprise.

"He is coming up the stairs to . . kill you!"

Just for a brief second the Earl stared at her as if he thought she was demented.

Then he said:

"If that is what you believe, we will make sure we are prepared. Go and hide behind the curtain!"

He pointed as he spoke to the window on the other side of the fireplace where the curtains were drawn.

Noella was too frightened to do anything but obey him.

She pulled the curtains to so that she could just peep through them to see what the Earl was doing.

He had got out of bed and to her surprise was pushing one of the pillows down beneath the sheets and blankets where he had been lying.

He placed another where his head had rested.

He pulled the sheets high and she realised that although the moonlight was bright on the floor inside the room, the four-poster bed was virtually in darkness.

She thought in her terror that the Earl was being incredibly slow.

He picked up the long dark robe which lay on the chair beside the bed and put it on.

Then he moved behind the curtain that was pulled back from the window.

She realised that where he stood he was now invisible.

Then there was complete silence.

Nothing moved and all that Noella could hear was her heart thumping in her breast.

It suddenly struck her that perhaps she had been mistaken and that Jasper did not mean to kill the Earl.

Perhaps at this very moment he was collecting the snuff-boxes and taking the miniatures from the walls.

Just when she felt that she had made a fool of herself and would find it difficult to explain how she had become involved, there was just the faintest sound outside the door.

She stiffened.

Peeping through the curtains she could just see the door moving slowly and silently open until Jasper came into the room.

He seemed little more than a dark shadow, and yet it was a shadow that moved steadily towards the bed.

He must have stood for only a second looking down at what he thought was the sleeping Earl, but to Noella it seemed like a century.

Then with his left hand he drew something from his pocket and dropped it onto the cover on the bed.

With his right hand he drew out a long, pointed dagger.

It flashed in the moonlight before he plunged it into what should have been the heart of the sleeping man!

It was then that the Earl stepped forward from his hiding-place to say:

"Good evening, Jasper! You are an unexpected visitor!"

Jasper started and recoiled as if the Earl had frightened him.

Noella could now see his face because the moonlight was full on it and he was almost ludicrous in his astonishment.

As he turned as if to run away, she saw that the Earl held a pistol in his hand.

"Not so fast!" he said, "I want an explanation of your behaviour!"

"If you kill me," Jasper retorted, "you will be charged with murdering an unarmed man!"

"You are hardly unarmed," the Earl said, "with your dagger thrust into what you believed to be my heart!"

"Prove it! Prove that I did it!" Jasper said jeeringly. "It was Noella who stabbed you, as I can prove in a Court of Law."

He shouted the words.

Because she was so surprised Noella moved forward from her hiding-place between the curtains as if to protest.

Jasper saw her and with a swiftness which took both her and the Earl by surprise, he pulled his dagger out of the bedclothes.

In one unexpected movement he had one arm around Noella's neck and the dagger pointing at her breast.

"Stop me, and I will kill her!" he said to the Earl and began to move backwards towards the door, dragging Noella with him.

"If you do not stop," the Earl said, "I will shoot what I can see of you, and as you well know, Jasper, I am a good shot!"

"If you want to protect her, then you can save your bullet," Jasper said. "She is not your sister, but a double-crossing little bitch!"

His words seemed to echo round the room.

He took another step and the point of the dagger pricked her breast.

As she gave a scream of pain and terror there was a violent explosion.

It was not a bullet fired by the Earl.

The sound came in fact, from behind Jasper, and as he collapsed onto the floor, Noella was free.

It was then she saw Hawkins standing in the doorway, a smoking pistol in his hand.

Chapter Seven

For a moment Noella stood immobile, deafened by the sound of the pistol and feeling as if everything was swimming in front of her eyes.

She put out her hand as if for support.

The Earl's arms went round her, and as he picked her up she knew she was alive and the terror was over.

For a moment she could only shut her eyes and feel thankful that he was safe.

Then she realised he had passed Hawkins and was carrying her out through the door and into the corridor.

When he reached her bedroom, he pushed open the door with his foot to take her inside.

He laid her down very gently on the bed.

As she looked up at him in the candlelight she knew at that moment, as if a voice had told her so, that she loved him.

Instinctively, because she knew he was going back to his bedroom, she held on to his robe saying:

"Do not . . leave me!"

"I must go to tidy everything up," the Earl said quietly. "I will come back later. In the meantime, Nanny must see to your wound."

Noella looked down.

The blood from the sharp point of the dagger with which Jasper had pierced her had seeped through her negligee and made a crimson stain.

The Earl pulled violently at the bell which hung beside the bed and rang in Nanny's room.

"Tell your Nurse to attend to you," he said, "but you are not to talk about this to anybody else."

Then before she could say anything he had gone and Noella was alone.

It was then for the first time she remembered that Jasper had told the Earl she was not his sister.

As the whole implication of his revealing the truth swept over her like a sudden tempest, she started to cry.

Tears ran down her cheeks as she told herself that now she would have to go away.

She knew that to leave the Earl would be agonising.

"I . . love him . . I love . . him!" she murmured in her heart.

Nanny, looking very strange in a woollen shawl covering her flannel nightgown, came into the bedroom.

"You rang your bell, Miss Noella?" she asked. "What's wrong?"

She saw the blood on Noella's negligee and gave a cry.

"You're bleeding! How can you have injured yourself?"

"It . . it was Jasper," Noella stammered.

Then as she realised he was dead and that Hawkins had killed him, the tears came even faster.

She knew that Hawkins could be taken to prison or, worse still, hanged.

How could this have happened? How could anything so terrible have occurred when she had been so happy?

Nanny did not talk, she merely in her usual efficient manner helped Noella out of her negligee and stained nightgown.

She washed away the blood from her breast seeing with relief that the wound was not deep.

She covered it with a pad of fine linen and held it in place with a bandage.

Then she gave Noella a clean nightgown and pulled up the bed-clothes.

Noella was like a puppet in her hands, not thinking of

anything except that the world had fallen into pieces around her.

When they were back in Worcestershire, she would never see the Earl again.

As she lay back against the pillows Nanny washed her face gently and dried it with a soft linen towel.

"Now stop crying, dearie," she said, "it'll heal quickly, and tomorrow we'll ask His Lordship to send for the Doctor."

"No! No!" Noella said in an agitated voice. "No one must know .. no one must have .. any idea .. what has .. occurred tonight."

"What *has* happened?" Nanny asked.

Noella could hardly bring herself to answer, then she said in little more than a whisper:

"Jasper .. threatened to .. kill me and .. Hawkins shot him .. dead!"

Nanny stared at her as if she had not heard her aright. Then she said in her usual tart voice:

"And the world'll be a cleaner place without him! Now, don't you worry yourself, Miss Noella. Just go to sleep and everything'll feel better in the morning."

Noella wanted to reply that it would be much worse, because then the Earl would send them away.

But it was impossible for her to speak because the words seemed to be in her throat.

Nanny was tidying away the bowl she had used to wash her wound, the towel and some blood-stained linen.

She picked up the discarded nightgown and negligee and put them over her arm.

"I'm going to leave you now, dearie," she said, "unless you'd like something to drink?"

"No. No .. I want .. nothing!" Noella replied.

She knew it would be a mistake for Nanny to go down to the kitchen and perhaps come in contact with one of the other servants.

"Then goodnight and God bless you," Nanny said. "I'll leave the candle in case His Lordship comes to see you."

Noella did not argue.

The Earl had said he would be back but she did not think he would remember.

It flashed through her mind that perhaps he was having Hawkins arrested.

More important he would first have to take Jasper's body out of his bedroom.

She had no idea what he would do about it. She only knew that now he would hate her because she had deceived him.

Never again would he talk to her so interestingly, or so pleasantly as he had done at dinner.

She wished she could leave before he told her to go.

But for the time being it would be impossible for her to dress with a bandage over her breast.

Anyway, they could not leave without a carriage to convey them.

She found herself thinking that perhaps, as Jasper had threatened, the Earl would throw them out without any luggage or money.

They would have to try to walk home and would starve on the way.

In her terror that this might really happen, she conjured up a picture of Nanny collapsing by the roadside.

Then Hawkins and herself would have to beg from passers-by for a few pennies to buy something to eat.

"I wish I were . . dead!" Noella thought.

Once again the tears began to run down her cheeks.

The door opened and although she knew who had come into the bedroom, she could not see him.

He came to stand beside the bed, and she waited for him to denounce her and order her as a liar to get out of his sight.

Then she felt him sit down on the bed facing her, and tentatively though still trembling, she opened her eyes.

"I thought you might be asleep," the Earl said in his deep voice, "but instead you are crying."

"Are you . . very . . angry?" Noella whispered.

126

The words were almost inaudible and looking down at her the Earl could see that she was trembling.

With her wet lashes, the tears on her cheeks, and the fear in her eyes she looked very pathetic.

He looked at her for a long moment before he said quietly:

"I expect you want to know what has happened."

"Will .. Hawkins have .. to stand .. trial?"

It was the first thing that came into Noella's mind.

She had no idea that the Earl thought it was characteristic of her to think of her servants rather than herself.

"Hawkins has gone with my Valet, whom I trust completely," the Earl replied, "to fetch the Chief Constable."

Noella gave a little cry of horror, but he went on:

"He is an old friend of my father's, and I have known him all my life. I think when he learns the whole story of what has occurred he will help us to cover up what would otherwise be a scandal."

"You mean .. because Hawkins .. killed Jasper?"

"I mean that Jasper attempted to murder me, and threatened to kill you!" the Earl said harshly.

There was silence, then Noella, as if she had to understand, asked:

"Are you .. saying there .. will be .. no trial .. and no one need .. know?"

"I think, in fact I am sure," the Earl said, "that Jasper's death will be put down as Misadventure, and he will be buried as a member of the family decently and respectably."

Noella gave a little sigh of relief and the Earl said quietly:

"Hawkins has told me that he discovered the new Pantry Boy had been bribed by Jasper to tell him if ever I went away."

Noella remembered thinking there must be a spy in the Castle.

"He therefore, and it was intelligent of him, was

suspicious of the note you received and followed you when you went to the Temple."

"I . . I had to . . go!" Noella said slowly.

"I realised that," the Earl said, "and Hawkins was clever enough to find out that as my Uncle Robert was dead, Jasper was now my heir presumptive and he had only to be rid of me to become the 6th Earl!"

"He . . meant to . . kill you!" Noella murmured in horror.

"And have you charged with it," the Earl said. "That is why he put your handkerchief on the bed beside what he believed to be my corpse."

Noella gasped and because the idea was so horrifying put out her hand towards the Earl.

He took it in his and the warmth and firmness of his clasp was very comforting.

It was horrifying to remember how Jasper had snatched her handkerchief from her pretending he had hurt his hand.

She realised it was a clever plot, and she might have found it impossible to save herself.

"But you saved me!" the Earl said very quietly as if he could read her thoughts.

"Suppose . . he had . . killed you?" she whispered.

"We are both alive," the Earl said, "and I can only thank you, Noella, for warning me as you did. But I wish you had told me he was blackmailing you."

Noella stiffened.

Now the moment had come when the Earl would accuse her of being deceitful and lying, and then he would throw her out as Jasper had said he would.

"I . . I am sorry . . I am . . terribly sorry," she murmured, "and I know you will never . . speak to me again but it . . seemed when . . Jasper suggested it the . . only way I could save Nanny and Hawkins from dying of . . starvation."

"And I imagine you too were equally hungry," the Earl remarked.

128

"It was wrong .. very wrong and .. wicked," Noella went on, "and Mama would have been .. shocked that I should have .. deceived you."

The tears choked her voice, then as the Earl did not reply she said:

"We will .. go away .. tomorrow, and perhaps .. one day you will .. forgive me."

"Does it matter to you," the Earl asked, "whether I forgive you or not?"

"Of course .. it matters, and I am ashamed .. deeply and abjectly ashamed of lying .. and I have always been desperately .. afraid that .. you would .. find out the truth."

"Yet I think there have been times when you were happy here," the Earl said.

There was a little silence before Noella said as if the words burst from her:

"Very .. very happy! I thought when we were .. riding together .. back to the .. Castle that if I ever .. had to leave .. it would be like .. being shut out .. of Paradise."

She could hardly say the last words for her sobs.

Then she felt the Earl rise and knew that he was leaving her, and perhaps she would never see him again.

The servants under his orders, would show her out of the Castle.

The humiliation would add to the misery she was feeling at being separated from him.

Then to her astonishment she heard him move, but not towards the door.

Instead he came round to the other side of the bed and lying down beside her put his arms around her.

He drew her close to him so that her head was on his shoulder.

She could hardly believe it was happening and yet when she opened her eyes he was there, lying beside her.

The strength and closeness of him was so wonderful that she thought she must be dreaming.

Then the Earl said, and his voice was very deep:

"Stop crying, my precious, and let me tell you what I feel about you."

Noella was so astonished that she opened her eyes and looked up at him, and realised how close his face was to hers.

She felt herself tremble, but it was not now with fear.

Instead there was a sudden hope in her heart like the first glimmer of an evening star.

Instinctively, without realising it, she moved a little closer to him.

"Now suppose we start at the very beginning," the Earl suggested, "and you tell me who you really are."

"I . . I am not . . your sister!"

"I am very glad about that!"

"You are? But I . . . ."

"Who are you?" he interrupted. "That is what must come first."

"I . . I am Noella Wakefield. My mother and your mother were cousins and were brought up together."

"So you are distantly related to me," the Earl said, "which is why, I suppose, you look like my sister."

"Noely and I might have been . . twins."

"What happened to her?"

"She . . died with . . her mother . . in our house in . . Worcestershire."

"Which is where I believe Jasper found you!"

"He came to find Noely . . and when he saw me . . because he wanted the money you had . . promised him . . he persuaded me to . . pretend to be your sister."

"I can hardly blame him for grasping at a unique opportunity," the Earl said unexpectedly.

Because Noella was afraid he was angry, she said again:

"I am sorry . . how can I tell . . you how . . sorry I am?"

"I know that is what you are feeling," the Earl replied, "but I also want you to tell me and truthfully, Noella, what you feel about me, not as your brother, but as a man."

130

She was shy, and finding it impossible to answer him she turned her head and hid her face against him.

"I want the truth – the real truth!" the Earl persisted.

Very gently he put his hand under her chin and turned her face up to his again.

"I . . I cannot . . tell you," she whispered.

"Why not?"

"Because it is . . something you . . would not wish to . . hear . . and it would perhaps . . shock you."

"I doubt if I would be shocked," the Earl said, "but I want the truth."

Because his hand was holding her chin and because his arm enveloped her, Noella felt as though she was no longer herself, but his.

Her terror and unhappiness seemed to be evaporating.

Instead there was a strange feeling as if the stars had come down from the sky and were flickering inside her body.

"Tell me the truth!" the Earl insisted.

Now she was vividly aware that his lips were very near.

"I . . I love you," she whispered at last, "I cannot . . help it . . but I love you . . and when I leave you . . I will . . want to . . die!"

She felt the Earl release her chin and his arm went round her as he drew her closer still.

Then his lips were on hers.

She knew as he kissed her that this was what she had longed for and thought she would never know.

It was as if the stars in the sky fell down and covered her, and their light was within her and flickering on her lips.

It was so perfect, so ecstatic, so much more marvellous than she had ever imagined, that Noella felt she must have died and was in Heaven.

Never had she imagined it was possible to feel such rapture, such incredible glory that could only have come from God Himself.

"I love . . you! I . . love you!" she said in her heart.

She knew the words pulsated through her whole body, and repeated and repeated themselves against the Earl's lips.

He kissed her until she was breathless.

Then he raised his head and asked in a voice that sounded strange and a little unsteady:

"How can you make me feel like this? How is it possible after all I have suffered to find that by a miracle you are not my sister?"

"Y . . you . . have suffered?" Noella questioned.

Because she felt so strange and unlike herself she could hardly speak, and it was even more difficult to understand what he was saying.

"I have loved you from the moment I first saw you," the Earl said. "I did not know that anybody could be so beautiful. When I realised that I was falling in love, although it might crucify me, I knew I had to send you away."

"Is that . . why you . . told me I had to . . marry Sir Stephen?"

"I thought at least you would be comfortable and provided for," the Earl said.

"But you were angry . . and very . . cruel to . . me!"

"How could I be anything else," he asked, "when you were driving me mad? Every time I looked at you I wanted to kiss you!"

She looked up at him waiting for him.

Then his lips were again on hers, and he kissed her demandingly, possessively and fiercely.

She was not afraid, even though she felt as if the fire in his eyes was on his lips and burnt her like the heat from the sun.

Only when he released her did she say once again:

"I love you! Oh . . Lyndon, I love . . you! But what . . can we do . . about it?"

"We are going to be married," he answered. "Then I shall know that I can never lose you!"

"How can . . you do . . that?" Noella asked in a

frightened voice. "So many . . people think I am . . your sister . . and I know you would . . hate a . . scandal."

"There will be no scandal," the Earl said firmly.

"But . . how . . how can we . . avoid it?" Noella asked.

"We will have to be clever, my darling," he answered. "Just as we are going to be clever about Jasper."

Because she had been carried away by the Earl's kisses, Noella had forgotten for the moment about Jasper.

Now, once again, he seemed to be there, menacing them.

"Leave everything to me," the Earl said. "There will be no need for us to stay here for Jasper's Funeral, which I shall arrange to take place very quietly with none of the family even being notified that he is dead."

Noella was listening.

At the same time, because she was afraid that something might spoil her happiness, she was holding onto the Earl and her face was raised to his.

"How can you be so beautiful?" he asked unexpectedly. "In fact, it is far more than that. It is everything you say, everything you do that makes me love you more, and I know it is impossible to live without you!"

"How can you . . say such things to me . . when I have been so . . deceitful?" Noella asked. "It should make you mistrust . . women . . even more than you do . . already!"

"I mistrusted women," the Earl replied, "because I missed my mother so terribly after she had gone, that I wanted to hate her for making me suffer."

Noella made a little murmur but did not interrupt.

"Then," he continued, "when you saved me from dying at Jasper's hands, I knew that you loved me as a woman would love her child. But now, my darling, I know you love me as a man."

"I love you . . so much," Noella said, "that there are . . no words in which to . . express what I am . . feeling."

She put up her hand to touch his face as if to make sure he was real. Then she said in a very soft voice:

"You know I would never . . hurt you, and I . . swear

before . . God I will never . . lie to you . . again."

There was nothing the Earl could do but kiss her, and it was a long time later before he said:

"In case the Chief Constable arrives to interrupt us, I must tell you of my plan."

"I want just to . . lie here and tell . . you how much I . . love you!" Noella said.

"And I want to be closer to you than that," the Earl replied.

Noella blushed and hid her face as he went on:

"I love you! God, how much I love you! But we have to try to be practical. It is important that you make no mistakes."

"I will do . . anything you . . tell me," Noella murmured.

"We will leave here tomorrow morning," the Earl said, "and go to London. We will be married very quietly in the Church nearest to my house in Park Street."

Noella raised her head to listen and he went on:

"Then we will leave to go abroad."

"A . . broad?"

Noella was surprised, remembering how he had raged against the places where his mother and Noely had lived.

She did not have to explain because he continued:

"We shall be travelling in a yacht which I know I can borrow from one of my friends who has offered it to me before."

He kissed Noella's hair before he said:

"I think, my darling, we shall enjoy exploring beautiful places which neither of us have seen, and which will give us new horizons and a great deal to talk about."

"It will be . . wonderful to be . . anywhere with you!" Noella said simply.

"A short while after we are married," the Earl said, "it will be announced that both the Countess of Ravensdale and her daughter Lady Noella Raven had died in Rome."

Noella looked at him enquiringly and he said:

"Those who are interested, and that will include the

Raven family, will think that I took you to meet my mother and that I was making my peace with her."

"That is clever of you," Noella murmured.

"We will travel until the autumn," the Earl went on, "and then just before we return, I will have it announced that I have been married to Miss Noella Wakefield."

"Do you think . . anyone will . . realise that it was I who pretended . . to be . . your sister?"

"Why should they?" the Earl asked. "The family will of course be aware that your mother and mine were cousins, and they thought you were. People see what they expect to see, so they will all be quite certain they have never met you before."

Noella gave a little sigh.

"That is very, very clever of you," she said. "But you are certain . . quite certain . . that you . . should marry me?"

The Earl laughed and it was a very happy sound.

"I am very, very certain that I intend to marry you, and nothing and nobody shall stop me!"

His lips were seeking hers again as he said:

"I adore you, my lovely one, and now at last I can say so, and not have to fight against my love which has been a losing battle!"

He kissed her again before he got up from the bed saying:

"I am going to dress and be ready for the Chief Constable. After that my Valet will start packing for me, and I suggest you wake your Nurse at about six o'clock and see that she and the housemaids pack everything you possess."

As the Earl spoke he walked across the room to pull back the curtains.

Noella could see now that the stars were fading in the sky and there was that hush over the earth which comes just before the dawn.

She knew that soon the first faint sign of the sun would appear in the East.

She knew that the Earl was looking out over his own land and thanking God that he was not only alive, but in love.

Then he turned and walking across the room said:

"Hurry, my precious one, I want more than I have ever wanted anything in my life for you to be my wife! But, remember until we leave here that you are my sister!"

Noella smiled at him and he thought it was impossible for any woman to look more radiant.

Then the door closed behind him and Noella lay back against the pillows saying over and over again:

"Thank You, God, thank You!"

The Earl and Noella travelled South in a comfort and luxury which seemed very different from the way she had come North with Jasper.

Now the Earl's large and very comfortable travelling-carriage was drawn by six horses.

When they changed them at Posting Stations, it was for a team of his own which had gone ahead to be waiting for them after they had spent a comfortable night.

The rooms may not have been very luxurious.

But the Earl travelled with his own linen, his own bedside rugs, his own wine and most of the food he required.

One of the outriders, and there were four of them, was an excellent cook.

His Valet and Hawkins thought of everything which might add to their happiness.

Nanny travelled with Hawkins and the luggage and when she was let into the secret that they were to be married, she cried from sheer happiness and said:

"His Lordship's everything your dear mother would have wanted you to have as a husband, and I know, dearie, His Lordship'll make you as happy as she was."

Noella could not help sometimes remembering that she might have had to marry Sir Stephen and shivered at the thought.

136

Yet now she knew how much the Earl loved her, she was sure that even though he had wished to put her out of his life he would not have deliberately made her unhappy.

"I was frightened of my own feelings," he had said when they talked about it, "and because Stephen Horton is so rich, I thought I was doing what was best for you."

"But you know . . now that I could not . . marry a man I did not love!" Noella said.

"I did not believe in love until I met you," the Earl replied. "At least, that is what I told myself. Now I know I was just afraid of suffering as I had because I loved my mother."

"You will . . never be . . unhappy again," Noella murmured.

When they reached London, the Earl sent Noella to bed immediately on their arrival knowing she would be tired after the long journey.

"I have a great many preparations to make," he said, "and because I am thinking of you, my precious one, I want you to sleep not only through the night, but for most of tomorrow. We are to be married in the evening."

Because, although she was so happy she was also rather tired, Noella said:

"I will do . . whatever you tell me . . to do. At the same time . . I want to be . . your wife."

"Not half as much as I want to be your husband," the Earl said, and she knew he spoke from his heart.

However, to please him she slept until very late the next day and when she awoke he had gone out.

She was certain it was to make arrangements for their wedding, and for the yacht which was to carry them on their honeymoon.

She could think of nothing more exciting than to visit strange lands she had never seen and be with the Earl.

"If we travelled anywhere," she thought in her heart, "just away into the blue . . it would be like being in Heaven . . so long as he was there!"

Nanny, who seemed to have become years younger because she was no longer afraid for the future, had chosen a lovely gown that Noella was to wear as a bride.

It was of course white and it came from a shop which the Earl had told her had the best gowns in the whole of London.

She found one of gauze trimmed with frills of lace that was more beautiful than any gown Noella had ever seen.

It had the large sleeves that were fashionable and Noella's tiny waist above the full skirt made her look as if she had just stepped out of a Picture-Book.

Because they were married in secret, and not even the servants in London were to know what was happening, Noella wore a bonnet trimmed with white roses.

Instead of a bouquet she carried in her hand a Prayer-Book with the cover made of Mother-of-Pearl.

She looked so lovely that the Earl felt he had no words in which to tell her of his feelings.

Instead as they drove in a hired carriage so that their own coachman would not know where they were going, they just sat in silence.

Their hands were clasped until the Earl kissed her fingers one by one.

Nanny had bought Noella some lace mittens to wear with the gown instead of the more conventional kid gloves.

As Noella felt the warm insistence of the Earl's lips, she felt herself quiver with sensations that were once again like the twinkling of the stars.

Only when the horses stopped outside the small Church where they were to be married did he say quietly:

"I worship you, my darling!"

The Church was very quiet and the elderly Parson spoke the words of the Service with a sincerity which was very moving.

The altar was decorated with Madonna lilies, which to the Earl symbolised the purity of his bride.

He knew, as if the Saints were telling him so, that she would never shock or disappoint him.

After the Priest had blessed them, they walked slowly down the aisle, and Noella was sure the angels were singing.

They drove back to the Earl's house and had a delicious meal in the Dining-Room which looked very different from how it had looked when Noella had stayed there on her way with Jasper to Yorkshire.

There were only Hawkins and the Earl's Valet to wait on them.

The silver had been brought from the safe, and the Earl had the dark oak pannelling hidden by garlands of flowers.

There were flowers on the table, and flowers too in the bedroom which Noella had never seen before.

She realised because it was so beautiful and so feminine that it had been the Countess's room.

She knew that in sleeping in it the Earl told her without words that he had forgiven his mother for deserting him.

He understood now as he had never been able to do before the irresistible power of love.

She thought that one day she would talk to him about it, but not tonight.

Perhaps not until they were so close that they would not only have no secrets from each other, but their thoughts would be formed as one.

Nanny helped her into bed.

Then when Noella lay waiting, she prayed that the Earl would not be disappointed in her.

She was afraid he would find her very ignorant where love was concerned.

Although he had admitted that he mistrusted and hated women, they had nevertheless been from time to time in his life, although he had no real love for them.

When he came into the room he looked, she thought, so handsome that she knew that whatever he had felt a great number of women must have given him their hearts.

He came to the bedside and sat down as he had before on the side of the bed.

"You are looking worried, my precious one," he said. "Tell me why."

"I . . I am a little . . afraid," Noella whispered.

"Of me?"

"No . . that I may . . disappoint you."

She put out her hands towards him saying:

"I realise how . . little I know about . . anything except . . the quiet countryside . . the flowers and the birds . . they are much more . . real to me than . . people."

She drew in her breath before she said in a very small voice:

"Suppose you . . find me . . boring?"

The Earl smiled.

"Do you think that possible?"

She thought he would kiss her lips. Instead he kissed first one of her hands, then the other.

Then taking off his robe, he got into bed beside her.

There was only one candle burning in a gold candlestick behind the silk and muslin curtains which fell on each side of the bed.

Noella could see his face very clearly, and she thought there was a touch of fire in his eyes as his lips sought hers.

He kissed her passionately but at the same time very tenderly.

Holding her close against him he said:

"I would not want you to be afraid, my darling, and I will be very gentle because you are so young and, thank God, so innocent."

"Also . . very . . ignorant!" Noella whispered.

"Do you think I would want you to be anything else?"

He pulled her even closer to him as he said:

"I suppose because I was disillusioned when I was so young, I have always secretly wanted to find a woman who knew nothing about love until I could teach her."

"When you . . have taught me . . supposing you are . . disappointed?" Noella asked.

"That is impossible," the Earl answered.

He put out his hand to smooth away the hair from her face and to run his fingers down the outline of her cheek.

"You are so exquisite," he said, "and no one could be with you, my precious, without realising you are as lovely inside as you are out."

He drew in his breath as he said:

"That is what I wanted, and now that you are mine, I will look after and protect you, and at the same time, worship and adore you for as long as we both shall live!"

The way he spoke made Noella realise it was a vow and she said softly:

"That is what I want, and that is what I too have . . dreamt I might find . . and I am very . . very lucky."

"I am lucky too," the Earl said, "although I think a better word would be 'blessed'."

His voice was serious as he said:

"As we were being married I felt that God had blessed us both in letting us find each other. We belong, my darling, not just in name and because your body will be mine, but also in our hearts and souls."

Because Noella had never thought the Earl, of all people, would say anything like that she gave a little cry of sheer happiness.

Then as her arm went round his neck to pull his head close to hers, she said:

"Oh, my darling, wonderful Lyndon, teach me . . teach me to be exactly as you want me to be! I love you . . I love you . . I love you with all my heart and soul!"

She knew the way she spoke excited the Earl and he drew her closer to him.

With his lips seeking hers she said in a whisper:

"There is . . something I want to . . say to you."

"What is it, my precious, my darling?"

His lips moved over the softness of her cheek down to her neck.

It gave her sensations she had never known before,

which were so vivid, so unbelievably exciting, that it was difficult to speak.

Yet she knew he was waiting to hear what she had to say, and after a moment she said:

"As you .. know .. I am very .. ignorant about .. love," she whispered, "except that it .. comes from God but .. because I love you .. I want you .. please to .. give me a son .. so that never again will I be .. frightened of heirs presumptive like Jasper, trying to .. kill you."

Because the Earl was still she thought perhaps she had said something wrong.

Then as she looked into his eyes she knew it was what he wanted to hear.

He was in fact, looking at her as if she was something not only very special, but also sacred.

His lips were on hers and he kissed her at first gently.

Then as if he could not help himself, he kissed her more demandingly, more passionately.

She felt as if the fire that burned in him had joined the starlight within her and turned it into fire.

It was the fire of purity which burned away evil, the deceit the lies and all that was wrong and wicked.

It was the fire of the Divine that was like the heat of the sun, and yet it was in itself everything that was pure and beautiful, like the glory of the flowers and the song of the birds.

Then as the Earl swept Noella through the gates of Paradise, she knew that their love given to them by God would go on unto Eternity.

OTHER BOOKS BY BARBARA CARTLAND

Romantic Novels, over 400, the most recently published being:
Forced to Marry
Bewildered in Berlin
Wanted – A Wedding Ring
The Earl Escapes
Starlight over Tunis
The Love Puzzle
Love and Kisses
Sapphires in Siam
A Caretaker of Love
Secrets of the Heart
Riding to the Sky
Lovers in Lisbon
Love is Invincible
The Goddess of Love
An Adventure of Love
A Herb for Happiness
Only a Dream
Saved by Love
Little Tongues of Fire
A Chieftain finds Love
The Dream and the Glory (in aid of the St. John Ambulance Brigade)

Autobiographical and Biographical:
The Isthmus Years 1919-1939
The Years of Opportunity 1939-1945
I Search for Rainbows 1945-1976
We Danced All Night 1919-1929
Ronald Cartland (with a Foreword by Sir Winston Churchill)
Polly – My Wonderful Mother
I Seek the Miraculous

Historical:
Bewitching Women
The Outrageous Queen (The Story of Queen Christina of Sweden)
The Scandalous Life of King Carol
The Private Life of Charles II

The Private Life of Elizabeth, Empress of Austria
Josephine, Empress of France
Diane de Poitiers
Metternich – The Passionate Diplomat

Sociology:
You in the Home
The Fascinating Forties
Marriage for Moderns
Be Vivid, Be Vital
Love, Life and Sex
Vitamins for Vitality
Husbands and Wives
Men are Wonderful
Etiquette
The Many Facets of Love
Sex and the Teenager
The Book of Charm
Living Together
The Youth Secret
The Magic of Honey
The Book of Beauty and Health
Keep Young and Beautiful by Barbara Cartland and Elinor Glyn
Etiquette for Love and Romance
Barbara Cartland's Book of Health

Cookery:
Barbara Cartland's Health Food Cookery Book
Food for Love
Magic of Honey Cookbook
Recipes for Lovers
The Romance of Food

Editor of:
"The Common Problem" by Ronald Cartland (with a preface by
the Rt. Hon. the Earl of Selborne, P.C.)
Barbara Cartland's Library of Love
Barbara Cartland's Library of Ancient Wisdom
"Written with Love" Passionate love letters selected by Barbara
Cartland